LOVE TO THE RESCUE

"Ze shredder is fun if it is handled er . . . correctly. Zat idiot was not in control of his apparatus and in ze wrong area. It is for advanced skiers only. Are you an advanced skier Miss, er . . .?"

'Apparatus'? What kind of species speaks like that? I got back to my feet and for the first time turned to look at the guy with the funny accent. My rescuer.

Then it happened.

My eyes connected with his and it was like being zapped with electricity. I was also totally unprepared for the really weird feeling that followed. I don't mean it wasn't unfamiliar—just the opposite.

It was love. . . . *I was in lerve!*

My Life as a Snow Bunny

Kaz Delaney

SMOOCH   NEW YORK CITY

For Heather (aka Holly Cook):
the biggest nag, most brutal crit partner
and best friend a girl could have.

SMOOCH ®

December 2003

Published by

Dorchester Publishing Co., Inc.
200 Madison Avenue
New York, NY 10016

ISBN 0-8439-5296-2

The name "SMOOCH" and its logo are trademarks of Dorchester Publishing Co., Inc.

Printed in the United States of America.

Visit us on the web at www.smoochya.com.

My Life as a Snow Bunny

Chapter One

I couldn't believe it! Me! Jo Vincent, the original California girl was actually standing ankle-deep in snow! Okay, so you have to substitute curly brunette hair for the usual long blond Californian locks to get the exact image. And maybe drop a few inches in height. And decrease a few curves. Okay, okay, it's a stretch.

Let me put it simply. Trivialities aside, the point is that I, the dedicated sun, surf, and sand freak, had made the never-before-considered transition and was at this moment tottering on brilliant, white, freeze-your-butt-off snow. And it was great!

It seems really lame now that I hadn't been all that keen to come. In fact, I'd fought it all the way. I'd figured that Dad's offer was one of those conscience-clearing things. You know: spend heaps of money on your kid to prove that she *is* loved despite the fact for most of the year the guy is too busy to lift the phone to dial seven digits.

I admit I am just bitch enough to make Dad have to work for my affection a bit harder than that. Does the guy really think I am so shallow that all he has to do is wave an airline ticket, four-star accommodation, and the chance to see some hot bods in action—and I'll come running? Oh, puleese!

Okay, okay. I admit I was tempted. I like to travel. And I looove room service. And I admit, too, that the opportunity of witnessing those hot bods in action *had* caused some serious weakening on my part. Until I remembered they'd all be in school. Eeoww. Stuck in the snowfields sandwiched between the nursery set and the geriatric set. Either way, I'd end up covered in applesauce. No way.

Me, shallow? Get a grip! He'd simply have to try harder than that. I wasn't going.

Mom was the one who convinced me. Yes, the real reason I was here could be laid directly on the altar of my mother's incredible powers of persuasion. She listened objectively to my tirade and my reasons. And uttered nine memorable words: "Go or I confiscate your surfboard for a year."

No surfboard?

It was a king hit. One slug and I was begging for mercy.

And thermal underwear.

Colorado, here I come. No argument.

She said Dad and I needed it. She said I'd love it. And it *was* only for a week. Way to go, Mom! I would have settled for a rabies shot.

That was then.

Now, I was shrugging off the injustice of the fact that mothers get more than their fair share of turns at being right—and just let the incredible scenery wash over me. This was cool. This was way more than cool.

Yeah. As I stood there looking out over those huge snow-covered mountains, the blue sky, at the trees dripping with sparkling icicles, I decided that I could force myself to enjoy this week. Even if it meant spending it with Dad and his latest. Besides, who argues with a week out of school? Everything has an upside, right?

I tested this newly discovered scenery through the viewfinder of my camera. Apart from the beach, that was my other passion—photography. I fiddled with the telescopic lens, closing in on the action seeming just inches away on the slopes. And as I zoomed in, my blood pressure zoomed up! Feeling suddenly weak at the knees I had to acknowledge that photography was just *one* of my other passions. Oh, my . . . I stood glued to the spot, absorbing the fabulous scene before me.

Guys! Hot athletic guys! The slopes were literally crawling with them.

My head shot up. Why hadn't I thought of that? If *I* was out of school, it stood to reason other kids could be out of school! I felt like smacking my forehead for having been so stupid. Guys and surf boards go together—why not guys and snow skis? Let me at 'em! Just how many upsides could one vacation offer, anyway?

I went back to the viewfinder. It was poetry in motion. *"How do I love thee? Let me count the ways. . . ."* I shook my head in disbelief. There was no way I could even *begin* to count all that scorching talent swerving and swaying on their skis.

I was mesmerized. Totally unable to break eye contact . . . It was only when I tried to sigh that reality finally kicked back in. My mouth wouldn't move. Oh, no! Had my drool frozen my lips together? Now, there's an attractive sight. Long strings of frozen drool hanging precariously like fangs bared for attack. That'd bring 'em running to me in droves!

I rubbed at my mouth furiously, glad to feel tingling warmth flowing back into my lips and hoping no one noticed what a dork I'd been. Just in case, I pulled myself up to my full, if barely adequate, height and tried to regain some dignity. I detest females who publicly salivate over guys, and reluctantly dragged my eyes away from the testosterone temple I'd been worshiping.

Okay. Regroup. I knew I was ready for them. I just wanted to charge right out there. But were they ready for me? Note to self: Plan a subtler strategy.

Back under control, I swung my trusty Kodak in the direction of the Chalet—my temporary home for the rest of the week. It was a good diversion.

Like most of the buildings at the newly created Pine Grove Ski Resort, the high-pitched roof with its fancy woodwork reminded me of a giant version of the gingerbread house in "Hansel and Gretel." Looking at the fairy tale image in front of me, I even had an idea who the resident witch might be. Not that I knew Kate Borelli very well yet. And not that it would matter. Not if Dad was still working at his usual turnover rate of female companions. Gone in sixty seconds. Well, almost.

Darn them! Now that I'd actually decided to enjoy myself I wasn't going to let them wreck this trip for me. With that thought, I determinedly concentrated on the shot, creeping backward as I angled for the wide view.

The place really was beautiful. All the buildings in the resort had been specially designed to resemble some authentic Swiss village. Not that I'd ever seen one in the flesh. But hey, I watch the Discovery Channel when there's nothing else on the teev!

Tiny flashes of light captured my attention. Tinsel sparkling in the sunlight—leftover Christmas decorations. Fir trees draped in colored lights that would twinkle against the white snow at night. I felt myself smile into the lens. Yep, this place was magic. . . .

Maybe magic was what happened next. For starters, the place had wound a spell around me. At least, that was my story. What else could I blame for being so totally unaware of what was happening? Because I swear I did *not* hear anything. Later I wondered how I could have missed the noise! It was like someone had turned on an electric ice crusher right beside me.

But at the time all I felt were a pair of strong hands grab at me—and propel me sideways. "Hey! What do you think you're doing? Hands off, spud! Put me down, you moron!"

"I vill do so ven it is safe!"

Safe? I twisted my head back from where I was being . . . well, *dragged* is closer to the description than carried—in time to see a guy on a kind of oversize skateboard minus the wheels whiz past me, way too close for comfort. That was just before the guy and his board parted company in a rather uncomfortable way, with him head-butting a sign half-covered by fallen snow. "Ouch! That had to hurt. . . ." I shook my head. "What *was* that wild thing, anyway?"

Danger over, my "rescuer" dumped me in the snow before answering, "Zis is called a 'shredder.' "

"A shredder? That's why the noise . . . Hey, that's cool! It kind of looks like fun! If you don't come off like that guy, that is. Can anyone hire one of those?" My eyes were still glued to the guy who was lying facedown in snow.

"Ze shredder is fun if it is handled, er . . . correctly. Zat idiot was not in control of his apparatus and in ze wrong area. It is for advanced skiers only. Are you an advanced skier, Miss, er . . . ?"

Apparatus? What kind of species speaks like that? The head-butt guy spluttered, shook his head, and climbed to his knees. He was okay. That out of the way, I got back to my own feet and for the first time I turned to look at the guy with the funny accent. My rescuer.

Then it happened.

My eyes connected with him and it was like being zapped with electricity. I was also totally unprepared for the really weird feeling that followed. I don't mean it was unfamiliar—just the opposite. In fact, I *recognized* it immediately from frequent past experience. What threw me was that I was just unprepared for it to happen so quickly. I sucked in my breath. It was like déjà vu. Face it—it *was* déjà vu . . . I knew this feeling well. In my sixteen years I'd experienced it, oh, at least fifty times.

It was love . . . I was in *lerve!*

My heart raced to try to keep up with my mind. This wasn't just plain old U.S. love—this was *lerve* with a Euro accent. This was steaming strudel . . . This was rich chocolate sacha torte . . . This was exotic . . .

Tingles wriggled right through me. This was high calorie lerve. . . .

I felt the sigh rumble up from way down deep.

My friends always joked that my only requirement for an eligible guy was that he had a pulse. They were wrong. My requirement for the perfect guy stood right here in front of me.

I guessed he was about my age, only he seemed heaps older—you know, more sophisticated. He wasn't all that tall, but that was okay, because I'm not very tall either. We were going to be perfect for each other.

I wondered if *he* realized that yet.

That accent had to be German, and that fit in with the blue eyes, white teeth, blond hair, and fabulous snow tan.

He was speaking to me again. "You still have not told me your name. Surely you are not shy? I cannot imagine someone with such sparkling eyes and pretty dimples vould be shy."

Sparkling eyes? Pretty dimples? The guy was really smooth. Could you imagine a guy from Franklin Vine High coming out with a gem like that? Actually it was a bit *too* heavy, even for my tastes, but perhaps he'd just discovered he was in love with me, too, and it was making him act all goofy. . . .

That had to be it.

I absolutely refused to accept the other possibility that was raging around in my head.

No alien could look this good.

That settled, I dazzled him with another beaming smile. It wouldn't hurt for me to do my bit for the good ol' U.S. of A. and deepen the relationship between it and . . . "Where are you from?"

"My home is in Switzerland." He actually clicked his snow boots together as he said it. I half expected him to goose-step back to his barracks. I was thankful he didn't. Goose-step or not, I didn't want him going anywhere just yet.

As for me, love makes you do weird things—like almost forget your manners. "Oops. You asked my name! Sorry. I'm Jo Vincent. And that was a really cool thing you did back there, saving me and all. Thanks!" Another dazzle. At this rate he'd need his eyes checked for high-wattage-smile damage.

I held the smile and idly supposed there'd be people who'd call my next words blatant.

I called it making the most of an opportunity.

"You know in some countries, if you save some-one then you own them. Does that mean that you own *me* now? You know, like you save me and then I devote the rest of my life to you?" I held my breath.

Had I sounded *too* eager?

He roared, laughing. It was a great sight; his laughter reached right up to his eyes, like he really meant it. I loved its warmth and the little creases at the sides of his mouth. Lordy, I *do* love being in love! And I was sure that deep down he was dying for me to devote the rest of my life to him, but he hid his disappointment well. I thought that showed character.

"That vill not be necessary, Jo; it vas my pleasure. And I am very pleased to meet you, I am Hans Gottlieb." He bent at the waist as he said it. Weird or not, every girl should have at least one Hans in her life. . . .

While he was bent over, I took advantage of those seconds to check out his bod. Not that it really mattered; when I love, I love totally and unconditionally. But still, it was a relief to find that the rest of him was okay on the eyes as well. The guy sure seemed well developed. I bet he had muscles on his earlobes.

But then again, I realized in sheer panic, he could be thinking the same about me! These suits might be terrific if you're five foot ten and willowy but if you're not . . . I mentally shrugged. I'm pretty much of a realist, and it's pointless whining about things you can't change. I was thankful there was one positive thing about this outfit: its bulk meant it kind of camouflaged my problem thighs. The downside was that you didn't notice my problem thighs because the rest of my body looked like one big problem.

Don't get me wrong: I'm not huge or anything close to it. But it's a sad fact that I just, like, don't suit bulky, shapeless clothing.

I flashed Hans another huge smile, really worked the dimples, and hoped that I dazzled him so much he'd forget to look down.

He was doing a bit of dazzling himself. I pegged his type pretty quickly: a totally rich tourist who would eventually carry me off to his love nest in the Swiss Alps, which would turn out to be this ancient romantic *schloss* (that's German for castle). Even the fact that I *knew* what a *schloss* was had to mean something.

It was a sign.

The longer I stared, the clearer the image became. He probably had royal blood. Yeah, it was getting clearer all the time. Prince Hans.

Princess Jo.

I think I'd take well to royal life. People to wait on me hand and foot. I was born for it. Mom could stop worrying about me being a slob—it was my destiny all along! I'd just been practicing all this time!

I sighed. Royalty. Blue blood. No denying it. It

was staring me right in the face. Breeding. You could always tell. I'm sooo good at reading people. . . .

It's a gift.

"So, I guess you're resting the crown for a bit? Whiling away your days in luxury here at Pine Grove? Or maybe for you, what we think of as luxury is actually, like, slumming it, huh?" Nudge. Wink.

He frowned. "Resting ze crown? I don't understand. Is this local terminology? But to answer part two of your question: No, no luxury for me, I'm afraid. I am vorking here as a ski instructor."

Ski instructor! Working!

"Oh, right. That was going to be my next guess. . . ."

"Pardon?"

"Don't worry about it."

It was okay. Like, I adapt really easily. Who needs servants anyway? Or crowns. They'd be a cow to surf in. "Hey, maybe you can teach me to ski? I've never been on skis, but I can ride a surfboard."

"Then I shall be honored to teach you. It is very fortunate that my job is to teach the beginners. But now if you vill excuse me, I must hurry to the office. I vill see you tomorrow, Jo, and I much look forward to it."

My smile was losing its dazzle. Did he have to go? The answer was obvious, because short of crash-tackling him, I had no legitimate reason to keep him here.

Bring on tomorrow! Meanwhile, he bowed again and flashed me one of his cute smiles.

As he hurried away another thought hit me, something else we had in common. Or, well, one thing at least . . . Wasn't the native tongue for Switzerland German? Or was it French? No, it *had* to be German! "Hey, Hans," I called, "I'll be able to practice my German on you. We can have all our conversations in German. Won't that be fun?"

Hans stopped tearing away as suddenly as if someone had just snap-frozen his feet in blocks of ice. He turned slowly, his face looking strange— frightened, even. Could word have spread this far, like across at least three states, that my German was less than perfect? So less than perfect that I was at the bottom of the class? Surely not. So then what?

"I'm so sorry, Jo, but I vould really rather speak English. You see, part of my reason for being here is to practice ze language. I hope you understand?"

"Sure, that's cool. See you tomorrow. 'Bye."

"Ya, it is cool. You must go in now and get warm."

I smothered a laugh and instantly understood why he needed to practice the language. Well, he could rest easy: I was the perfect person to help him!

Swinging my camera around my neck, I wandered back up toward the Chalet thinking about this great place. It was truly magic. It was sort of cold, yet it wasn't. It was hard to explain. Like, here I was surrounded by frozen air crystals and yet the sun was shining and I could feel my nose getting a bit burned!

And then there was Hans. . . . Where else would you find someone like that?

I did a little Snoopy dance in the snow. I'd been here barely one hour and I was in love already! Was that a record or what! "Let it snow, let it snow, let it snow!" Was that me singing Christmas carols in public in late January? Who cared!

My cell phone burned in my pocket. I couldn't wait to tell my friends, and started practicing just how I'd spin it. First thing when I got inside I'd text-message them all.

Then I froze. Literally.

What if I couldn't get cell reception here? An image of me trapped here for a whole week without a cell phone flashed across my mind. It wasn't pretty. Kind of like when someone has starved to death.

Shuddering, I bounded up three steps—not bothering to look up—and crashed straight into something hard. My head spun upward and I crashed again. But this time only my insides were affected. I was looking straight into the smiling face of another hunk! Man, this was paradise! Hunk heaven! Could love strike twice in a mere twenty minutes? Maybe I should consider a permanent move to the snow states!

This one had snagged me well and good. We'd obviously been about to collide, and he'd put his arms out to catch me and just happened to leave them there, wrapped around me. He was older than Hans and bigger, but what I could see of his face that wasn't covered with sunnies looked pretty cute.

I smiled back. "Sorry! My head was somewhere else. I didn't even see you."

His arms stayed around me. "No prob, babe." His smile—which on closer inspection I recognized to be a stupid grin—stayed in place as well, but the hands were moving lower down over my backside.

"Yeah, well, thanks. Gotta go. 'Bye!" I wriggled to get free but the arms held tighter. "Look, I don't want to seem like a bad sport or anything, but could you let me go?"

Still the stupid grin. It wasn't as though I was really frightened. I mean, we were on the steps of the Chalet in full view of the world. But I *was* starting to pick up some bad vibes. I didn't feel good.

Trying not to act like too much of a loser, I struggled a bit harder, this time knocking his sunglasses askew.

That's when I knew that maybe I *should* have been frightened.

Unlike Hans's eyes, this guy's eyes and smile weren't even on the same map, never mind reaching each other! The eyes were bloodshot and not focusing properly. My guess was that he was off his face—not in a major way, but high enough on something to be a pain in the butt.

A genuine oxygen thief. A loadie.

I hate guys like that—they're trouble.

"You're pretty cute," he said.

"You're not. And your eyes are giving me way too much information. Back off!"

Anger gave me the extra strength to push out of his grip and race up the steps. He obviously thought the whole episode was hilarious; I could hear him laughing until I shut the wooden door in his face. Moron!

Silently I hoped that was the last time I met up with that creep, but then an awful thought came to me: We'd met on the steps of the Chalet. Did that mean he was visiting? A shiver rippled down my spine. Or was he a Chalet guest as well?

Chapter Two

I leaned against the closed door to let my heartbeat return to normal. Jeez Louise!

A fire was crackling in one of the sitting rooms, and when my legs could support me without letting me fall flat on my face, I moved farther into the Chalet's foyer and poked my head into that room.

The voice startled me for a second. "Where have you been? I hope you're not going to mope around all week, Josephine. A lot of planning went into this trip."

That was my father speaking. I was still feeling spooked after my close encounter of the worst kind outside, and it momentarily soothed me to see him sitting on his own by the fire. I say *momentarily* because as soon as the words were out, I remembered who he really was. . . .

The Iceman.

Actually it was only the fact that he used the name Josephine, which I hate and Mom never calls me, that I even knew he was talking to me. The whole order was issued while his head was stuck in some business magazine. He didn't look at me once.

Calmer now, I struck a dramatic pose by the fireplace. "Well, actually, I met this Swiss count and we made mad, passionate love in the snow, and now I'm going to have his love child."

"Well, just as long as you remember that I expect you to have fun."

I narrowed my eyes. "Fun? Not sure I can guarantee it, Dad. The child will bring disgrace to the entire royal house, and I'll probably be kept in a dungeon and treated like a prisoner. Beaten. Fed only bread and water . . ."

"Hmm?" he grunted absently. "Good, that's more like it."

I stood in front of him for several minutes, hoping that he'd realize what I'd said and that I could get a reaction. Just once.

It had always been like this. He never listened. He yelled and ordered and controlled, but he never, ever listened. Inside I started shaking all over, this time from anger. I wanted to blurt out that I'd almost been molested on the steps but I couldn't. If he ignored that, too, I'd just die.

Like he'd read my mind, Dad looked up. He seemed surprised I was still there. "Why are you looking at me like that? You know, Josephine, I don't like your attitude of late. As your father, I have responsibilities, you know."

I held up one hand. Enough was enough. "I wouldn't go there, Dad. I might be forced to remind you that for the past three years you've hardly qualified for the Father of the Year award."

Would you believe it? The guy actually had the nerve to look bewildered! Like he had no idea what I was talking about! Then he just shook his head like it was all my fault and went back to his magazine. Sheesh! I stood there for a few more minutes, but obviously my command performance was over. He was finished with me. No explanations. No apologies.

I thought I was over crying for my dad, but there must have been a few tears left deep down—and they were about to make an appearance. I couldn't let him see that. I wouldn't let him see that he'd hurt me. Again.

Vision blurry, I turned to go. And came face-to-face with Kate.

Poor Kate—I'd hated her on sight. I mean, who wouldn't? She was tall, gorgeous, and she had this really cool job as a research analyst. I wasn't sure what that was—but she got paid big bucks to do it, so it must be cool. Not that I could hate her for that. It was just one of the things that made up the package.

Like the fact that she was thin.

No problem thighs there! And that her hair was dark and straight and silky—and cut to a bob at her shoulders. Apart from the fact that mine was dark and curly, frizzy even, another reason to hate her was that somehow *her* hair always seemed to hang just perfectly. And mine never did.

And she had my father's attention and I never do.

But despite my resolve, it was hard to hate the kind, gentle eyes that were staring back at me right now.

I wondered how long she'd been there. The last thing I needed was to have someone see just how unimportant I was to my own father. Or suffer someone's pity. I put my head down with only one intention—to make the bolt, and fast.

I think she tried to speak to me when I rushed past, but I didn't really give her much of a chance. But when I got to the stairs leading up to the bedrooms and looked back in, I could see Kate, and she seemed to be roasting Dad. The hardest bit for me to swallow was the fact that Dad was sitting there with this really lost look on his face, just as if he didn't have a clue what she was on about.

Good one, Dad.

I don't know why I was letting Dad get to me all

of a sudden. It wasn't like I wasn't used to the way he acted. And since he and Mom got divorced three years ago I hardly ever saw the guy. I was getting fairly used to not having him around. Mom and I are a pretty cool team; we look out for each other. We don't need him.

There was one thing I agreed with him on, though, and that was the fact that he'd spent heaps on this trip. This private chalet had only six guest rooms, and I'd seen the prices on a brochure in the lobby. It was one of the most expensive chalets in the resort. Dad had booked a suite for him and Kate and this room for me. And mine had four beds in it. Four beds and I had it all to myself!

Great.

Four empty beds.

Just what I needed to remind myself of my empty life.

For a minute as I flung myself down on one of them, I wished I'd been able to bring a friend or Mom.

But then I remembered Hans. I sighed. It would be tough, but I'd make do. The sacrifices a girl has to make . . .

They say that cool air sharpens the appetite. Whoever the mysterious *they* are, unfortunately they are dead right.

For someone who spends her whole life on a

diet, the aromas wafting up from the dining room at dinnertime were pure torture. There was no way I could fight them. Sometimes the body just totally overrules the mind. So it was with a sigh and a promise to live on bread and water for the rest of my life that I wandered downstairs.

Kate stood out as soon as I entered the room. In her tan suede designer pants, black ankle boots, and cream silk shirt, she made me feel pretty ordinary in my clingy purple sweater and jeans. The woman had style; I had to hand it to her. I had style too. My mother says they just haven't identified the type yet.

I'd tied my hair back with a black ribbon, but already I could feel little curls escaping. Hers hung like a silken curtain. Whoever the *they* were who claimed that "life's a crock" weren't wrong either!

She was standing watching He Who Will Be Obeyed. Dad seemed oblivious to her gaze, and was sitting at a long table with some other people. I could see why he'd zoned Kate out. I'd seen it all before—too many times.

Dad the businessman.

He was involved in a backslapping and hearty-laughing routine with this other guy. No prizes for guessing that this guy was a businessman like Dad. Good old Dad. Some things never changed. My old man could spot a clone of himself a mile away. I think they sniff each other out like skunks. Something about that image was suddenly appealing . . . it would help pass the time.

I watched for a few more seconds before letting out a low groan. *Something* was certainly needed to help me pass the time! They didn't even *grade* embarrassment to the depths I was feeling at that moment. Dad was worse than usual, really sucking up to this guy in the worst way. I slipped into a chair, for once not caring if he didn't notice me.

No such luck.

"Frank, Cynthia, I want you to meet my little girl, Josephine. Isn't she everything I told you she'd be?" He turned to me, "Honey, this is Mr. and Mrs. Woods."

"His" little girl! Someone pass me the puke bucket! "Jo," I corrected quickly in answer to the intro as I shook hands. Dad was big on manners.

"And this is their son, Justin," Dad continued. "Justin's on a break from Harvard."

I hadn't seen the other guy sitting at the end of the table. Pity. I knew Dad expected it, so I shook hands with Justin as well, but even before our hands touched I knew he was bad news. Sitting in front of me was the octopus-handed pothead I'd hoped never to lay eyes on again. Great.

I couldn't really blame Dad for being fooled. The guy looked okay. Ordinary. No signs hanging around his neck warning unsuspecting girls to give him a wide berth. No health warnings. He was sort of tall, with brown hair, and he had that great-skin-great-tan-great-teeth look that most rich kids have. I've always wondered where their folks go to buy them that stuff. . . .

Dad was still going on. "The Woodses have come here every season to ski since the resort opened. Mr. Woods is an investor in this place. He knows a good deal when he sees it. Eh, Frank?" More laughing and rib digging followed. Frank was obviously my dad's main man.

I was staring at the fire when the mutual admiration session finally wound down to something less nauseating. Just in time. Much more and I'd be completely off my food.

Then Dad spoke to me again and I seriously considered passing on the main course completely. "Josephine? You and Justin should get together. You and he would have a lot in common."

All I could do was stare at my father—the guy had obviously lost all his marbles. This I *could* blame him for. I mean, even my dog would be more clued in to exactly how much Justin and I had in common. Like, totally nothing! For starters, he was at college and I was in my junior year at high school. Hellooo? Like, doesn't that tell you anything? Then he's from the East and I'm from the West. Like Venus and Mars. And how about the fact that he skis every year and I've never had even *one* of my size six-and-a-half narrows on a ski in my entire life! And let's not forget the big one—I was not a druggie and he was.

Of course, this monologue was being played out entirely in my head. Dad heard nothing of it. But still, I didn't think it took a genius to work out that the way I saw it, the only thing Justin and I had in common was the fact that we were both members of the human race. Although in Justin's case even that was doubtful!

I wanted to shout, "Good one, Dad!" I didn't. Instead, like a dutiful daughter, I just smiled.

Fatal mistake! The snake smiled back, except that it was one of those smiles that sends warning bells clanging in your head.

My instincts were right about Justin Woods. Here we were sitting right under my father's nose and he was giving me the come-on. It was sickening, like he expected that I would never be able to resist him.

As if.

Suddenly before my eyes all those good looks vanished and I saw this slimy python sitting there instead. His head bobbed from side to side, his forked tongue darted in and out of his dry, flabby mouth, and his close-set, beady eyes stared coldly. I shook my head to dispel the image.

Pity. It'd been an improvement.

He was so smug—so superior. I can tell you now that the only reason he didn't end up wearing the delicious minestrone soup that had just arrived was because he wasn't close enough for me to orchestrate it. That and the fact that Dad would have killed me. I'm no wimp, but self-preservation is still high on my list of things to aim for.

The rest of the night, apart from the food, was definitely downhill. Occasionally Dad and Mr. Woods beamed at me as if they'd just given me a prize. And Justin the Jerk kept acting as though he *was* the prize and deserved the title. He must have thought that this whole scene was a great joke. After all, I blow him off in the afternoon; then in the evening my father practically hands me to him on a platter. Complete with an apple stuck right in my mouth.

Or maybe it was more like offering the mouse to the serpent. Yeah, well, ol' Justin was in for a big surprise, 'cause this mouse had sharp teeth and intended to use them if necessary!

At least I didn't have to deal with any of his rude comments. Even though he kept leering at me, he didn't have much to say. He was probably too out of it to put together a sentence. I wondered why the 'rents hadn't noticed and figured it was one of those cases where people saw only what they wanted to see. Parents can be like that.

I looked around at the others. Mrs. Woods was nipped, tucked, and polished to within an inch of her life. She looked like the prototype for the latest girlie toy.

Liposuction Barbie.

She was totally bored. And Kate? Well, Kate looked kind of upset.

One person I didn't have to worry too much about after those first humiliating moments was Dad. He ignored me, as usual, for the rest of the meal. He was too busy with his new best friends. And for the second time in my life I was grateful.

That's why I was caught totally unprepared when I heard, "Well, Justin, what do you think of my little girl? Didn't I tell you she was a cutie?"

Cutie? That was it—I'd had enough! Next Dad would be asking me to roll over and play dead or sit up and beg. His pet on show.

Part of me screamed silently that I probably wouldn't mind too much if I thought for one moment that Dad meant even one syllable! But I knew far better than to ever believe that. This was business. Mr. Woods obviously meant some kind of deal to my dad—and I was to be the pawn. Sorry, Daddy-o. I don't do party tricks.

I cut short any answer Justin was about to make by announcing, "I'm exhausted. I'm going to bed." I sounded rude and abrupt—and I didn't care.

Dad didn't look pleased. *Tough.* "Josephine, we're going to have a drink with the Woodses, and we thought you and Justin might want to try out the game room."

I bit my tongue. I bet I knew just what games Justin would want to play.

In the end I didn't have to say anything; it was Kate, of all people, who rescued me. "She's had a long day, Mal. Two flights and a different altitude and climate . . ." She seemed to be sending him a message I didn't understand, but I didn't complain, because it worked. I was off the hook.

But I'd only just gotten into my room when someone knocked. Uh-oh! This was it—Dad was sure to want to blast me for my unsociable behavior. My father always used to say that if you can conduct yourself socially, you can achieve anything. I figured now was when I was about to find out that I'd failed. Again.

Warily I opened the door. "Kate!"

"I hope you don't mind my coming up, Jo. I know you're not a child, but I just wanted to make sure that you were okay."

"Oh." What do you say to a witch who's suddenly turning into the good fairy? "Yeah, right . . . um, thanks . . . Come in."

She closed the door and sat on one of the beds. Looking around, she shook her head. "If I'd realized that this is what your father had booked for you, I'd have suggested to him that you bring a friend."

"I'll manage. Um, thanks for what you did downstairs." I was trying. Really trying. I would have to have been deaf, blind, and stupid not to see that she was a nice person—it was just that it was still really hard to see my parents with anyone else but each other. Even if my dad was a dropkick sometimes . . . No, make that *most* of the time.

Out of the blue she asked, "What do you think of Justin?"

"He gives me the creeps in a major way."

"Hmm, I thought that was the case. I don't think your dad meant to push you at him; he just—"

"Oh, come on, Kate! You heard him down there—I felt like I was a cow or something at an auction! And I absolutely detest being called cute!"

She tried to smother a little smile. But she wasn't quick enough. I knew that smile. It's the one adults give when they think you're too young to understand the point. Dad had made an artform out of it.

And I hated it.

"Thanks for nothing!" I muttered through clenched teeth. "Excuse me! It's time for me to have a shower!"

She grabbed my arm. "Wait, Jo. I'm sorry; I didn't mean to hurt you. That was really cruel of me to laugh. I remember what it was like to be a teenager, and all the insecurities it brings."

Yeah, well, like I was really going to fall for that one. I bet that Kate Borelli's face wasn't game to grow one zit when she was a teenager, let alone suffer from anything but a major case of being too beautiful. I didn't have to use words; I simply rolled my eyes in disgust. She got the message.

"It's true, Jo. My Italian mama believed that no self-respecting man would look at her daughters unless they had plenty of womanly curves. I'm tall for an Italian, and the result was that I ended up looking like a horse! I'd have given anything to have been called cute."

"Yeah, well, that was you. This is me and I hate it! So *your* feelings really have no relation to what *I'm* feeling."

She sobered. "You're right. But I hope one day you let me say, 'I told you so.' Because you really are a beautiful girl, Jo."

Whatever else I've been, I've never been vain, mostly because I'm basically honest. But Kate seemed sincere, so I figured I had two choices: believe that she really saw some potential or question her eyesight!

I wondered how someone found out about getting someone else a Seeing Eye dog?

Kate was pretty smart; she grinned before letting me know that she'd read my mind. "Okay, so I haven't convinced you. We'll see!" She laughed again. "But for now, please believe that I'd like to be your friend, and if you need anything this week, well, you know . . ."

She gave me a brief hug as she left, and while a part of me wanted to shove her away, another part felt her warmth. And it felt good. It made me miss my mom. Kate'd make a good mom someday.

"Lock your door," she whispered as she left. Yep, she'd be a very good mom.

I felt better after her visit. It made me calmer and able to think about a lot of things. The setting helped. Lying in bed was the most incredible experience—it was almost spiritual. Oh, I don't mean that it made me want to race out and find a church or anything, but cuddled up under big fluffy duck-down quilts, right under the uncovered window watching these beautiful white snowflakes falling down out of the black sky certainly made me really think about the mysteries of life.

"The mysteries of life . . ." That was one of my mom's favorite sayings about things she couldn't understand.

I seemed to have run into a few of those little mysteries myself today. Like Kate. The few times I'd actually spent with Dad in the past couple of years, his girlfriends had treated me like I had the plague, but Kate was different. It was still not like I really knew her or anything, but it was getting harder to dislike her.

And then there was Dad and Justin.

If Dad was really dumb enough to think that I could actually go for a loser like Justin, then we were in even more trouble than I thought.

But then I thought of Hans. No mystery there. The guy was my man—no sweat. The one minor problem that I could see was convincing *him* of that fact. *YM* magazine says that guys are pretty slow when it comes to recognizing the real thing. Oh, well. I supposed I was going to have to dazzle him with my fancy skiing. Then he'd never be able to resist me.

My last mental images as I drifted off to sleep were of me, decked out in the most fabulous ski gear, speeding down the slopes, every hair in place. The crowds were cheering. Flags were waving. . . .

And there was Hans waiting for me at the bottom of the slope. He didn't say a word; he didn't have to. His eyes said it all. Hans Gottlieb had recognized the love of his life.

Ace skier Jo Vincent . . .

Chapter Three

From when I was little, I'd always wished dreams could turn into reality.

Not anymore. Mine had just turned into a nightmare. It was the next day and we were on the beginner slopes.

Still.

"Vould you like some help?"

"No! I just want you to go away and leave me here to die!"

That was me. Not that Hans could hear or understand anything I'd said. How could he? My legs were at perfect 180-degree angles from my body, with long useless sticks of fiberglass stuck to the ends of them! My backside was sticking up in the air like a monument to clumsiness. And my face was buried in twelve inches of cold, wet snow. To say my words were muffled was an understatement. They'd been directed somewhere toward China.

To add to my humiliation, my ex-hero, Hans, was laughing! Oh, he wasn't doing it to my face, but I'd seen it in his eyes all morning, and I could hear it in his voice now. There was absolutely no doubt that this was *the* most embarrassing moment of my entire life. And he was loving every second of it.

Perhaps I should reconsider my decision to love him unconditionally for all eternity.

There's nothing like loss of dignity to send true love sour. It's as easy as leaving milk in the sun. That was me at the moment: milk in the sun. Totally useless.

I let my body flop deeper into the snow. What was wrong with me? Why was I such a klutz? I just could *not* believe that I wasn't handling this ski scene. I'm a surfer, for gosh sakes! To make matters worse, when we started out this morning these rotten little dudes who were about eight or nine years old had the same lessons that I'd had and now they'd gone off bunny hopping or whatever it is and even moved to higher ground!

But not me. Every time Hans said, "Knees together," my skis turned up at the ends like crossed swords ready for battle and sent me back onto my backside! Or front side. Every side but up.

Like right now.

Gloved hands grabbed me from behind and

started dragging me back onto my feet. Or my skis.

Despite feeling like the biggest idiot ever, I *was* kind of grateful. I mean, moments ago I'd been half-serious about his leaving me there to die. Then it had seemed like a better idea than having to face him again—ever.

But that was when I had humiliation at its highest degree burning through me to keep me warm. Now I was starting to freeze. Call me picky, but as more cold seeped into my body, I decided that there must be more comfortable ways to die from embarrassment.

Ways that didn't include snow and ice.

Or painful, unnatural positioning of body parts.

Back on my feet, I avoided eye contact with him. But he still wasn't going to make it easy on me. He kept at it. You gotta admire the guy's determination. Must be that Swiss blood.

"Come on, Jo; let's try again. Bend your knees and move your veight slightly forward. Let your veight carry you, slowly, gently. . . ."

Concentrate on Hans's words, I told myself silently. *Hang loose. Pretend you're on a surfboard. . . .*

"I'm doing it! Look, Hans! I'm doing it!" And I was. Of course, it lasted for about a full sixty seconds—but it was a start. And man, what a feeling!

Hans agreed. He knew what I was experiencing. I looked up and saw this fabulous smile plastered across his face and knew that I'd forgiven him for being a traitor earlier. It was such a great smile, like he was really pleased for me. There was just something about the guy, like, I don't know . . . like you could really trust him or something. Like he made you really want to be with him. Even without the cute accent he would have been irresistible. To me, anyway.

A big, sappy sigh rose right up from way deep inside me and plopped out. He was definitely my guy! Again.

"I knew you vould do it, Jo. Now ve just need to practice, and then maybe you can graduate from Flat Grove and move on to the next stage."

"Where's that?" I was ready. The fact that I'd actually only stayed upright for barely a minute wasn't even considered. Take me to the top of the mountain!

"It's called Sun Ridge. It's a medium-skill trail, and ve vill have to go up on the ski lift . . . but ve must practice some more first. Maybe you can be ready for tomorrow."

And practice we did, so much that by the time we climbed on board the last courtesy bus back to the village I was absolutely exhausted. But I was still determined that I was going to make it to Sun Ridge the next day. I had to prove to Hans that I wasn't a complete klutz.

"And so, Jo, vot did you think of your first day of skiing?"

"It was great. Of course, it'll never take the place of surfing. There is absolutely nothing like that feeling of soaring down the face of a wave that's closing over you. It's just you and it. You against nature."

"But Jo, zis is exactly like skiing. Ze speed, ze wind in your face, your heart beating so fast. Ze sound of ze skis as zey cut through ze ice . . ."

"Hey, you really get off on skiing, don't you?"

"Probably ze same as you 'get off' on zis surf riding."

"Yeah, I suppose you love skiing as much as I love surfing. I can certainly understand that."

The bus ride wasn't very long, but the swaying was making me sleepy. Man, I couldn't remember feeling this tired after a full day on the waves. I struggled to stay awake.

I mean, here I was with the man of my dreams sitting right next to me, and I was completely blowing the opportunity to make sure he knew that. And that he finally realized he felt the same way. "You know, Hans, all day long you've asked me heaps of questions. Hey, you know, I think you know my whole life story! And yet you haven't told me anything about you." Somehow I managed to get out the entire thing between yawns.

He didn't jump in to answer right away. I focused

Kaz Delaney

hard on keeping both eyelids in the open position
and stared at him.

Hmmm. You know I'm not really the suspicious
type, but even in my semi-docile state I was getting
the feeling that for the second time Hans looked
nervous. Even a bit scared. If I hadn't been so tired
I might have been worried about his weird reaction.
But to be fair, he'd been really kind and patient all
day, so I put it down to the fact that I'd worn him
out. And who knew? Maybe there was some nerv-
ousness because he was in a strange country.
Maybe his life was very different from mine and
maybe he didn't know how I'd take it.

And deep down I couldn't shake the idea that
maybe he really *was* royalty and couldn't tell me
for security reasons. Maybe he'd surprise me when
he announced our engagement.

One thing no one can ever doubt of me is my
optimism. You can't blame a girl for keeping all her
options open.

"Vot more could you vant to know?" he finally
answered. "I am seventeen, I am from Switzerland,
and I love to ski."

Heaps of things! I wanted to know everything!
Like, *Tell me about your folks, your family, your
house, your friends.* But not one word made it from
my mind to the outside world.

Not for lack of trying. But suddenly it seemed
everything was working against me. My own body

was betraying me. Not only would my eyes not stay open, but my mouth was refusing to operate—a problem *never* experienced by me before. I couldn't talk! I knew some teachers who would have paid real money to see me in this state. My mom would have mortgaged the house!

The bus reached the village, but by that time my exhaustion was so great that I didn't even have the energy to worry about Hans or whether he was madly in love with me yet. Or whether I'd be fitted for my own crown or just inherit a hand-me-down.

My major worry was how I was going to put one foot in front of the other for the walk up to the Chalet. It wasn't that far, but it was all uphill. Maybe I'd just have to stay on the bus, because I had this really wild feeling that none of my body parts would ever function again.

"Jo, ze bus has stopped. Everybody has already gotten off. Ve must go."

Even my eyeballs were in trouble. I couldn't focus on his face. "Oh, no," I managed to croak, "I think I must have caught some killer disease. I'm dying. . . ."

I heard him laugh; it sounded a long way away. "Zis is normal, Jo. Skiing or even just learning to ski is very hard vork. And of course, there is the altitude. It can be very tiring. Come; I vill help you to ze Chalet."

The only good part about this situation was that

I got to kind of lean all over him as he pulled me up the hill. Maybe I was too tired to notice, but he didn't seem to mind that much. "I am sorry that you are so tired, Jo. I was going to ask if you vould share a hot chocolate with me later."

The words hit like a wipeout.

This couldn't be happening to me!

I would have given a year—no, let's get real here—I would have given a month of perfect waves for one tiny scrap of energy. I was desperate. I willed my body to respond.

Nothing.

A corpse would have registered a higher activity readout! By this stage, Hans was acting like my Seeing Eye dog; I didn't even have the strength to open my lids. Life had never been so cruel!

I didn't even remember getting into bed. Later, I figured that Kate had had a hand in that, but at least one good thing came out of all this: I didn't have to put up with that slimy Justin.

Morning brought consciousness and two other sensations. The first was that life as I knew it was over.

I would never surf again. Worse—I would prob-ably never even walk again! My body would never recover.

And the second was that it wouldn't matter anyway, because I was starving to death by the moment!

Tummy growls that must have been echoing through the entire valley eventually prompted me to test the damage to my bruised muscles. I wondered if maybe just by some miracle I actually could survive the trip downstairs to breakfast. Then I thought of Hans and his promise to take me up to Sun Ridge.

It's amazing what strength a girl can find when her future with a guy is involved.

The fabulous mouthwatering smell of crisply fried bacon and fresh coffee provided the final motivation a little while later as I hobbied down the stairs. Hunger must have addled my brain, because when an arm suddenly wound itself around my waist I ignored the instinct to push its owner down the remaining stairs. Instead I twisted away—and winced at the pain.

"Hands off, Justin."

"I didn't see you pushing that guy away last night when he brought you home. . . ."

"Need to get your jollies spying on other people, do you? Well, for your information that was my instructor, and he was helping me because I was so tired!"

"And I wonder what you were doing to get so tired?"

I'd had the guy pegged from the first time I saw him. "You're pathetic!"

He didn't seem to care that I thought that he was disgusting; he just went on as though I hadn't spoken. The truth probably was that he'd heard that kind of response so many times that he didn't even notice anymore! "Who is this guy, anyway?"

I was just as stupid as he was for answering his question; he didn't deserve the breath I was wasting on him. Two things helped; one was that he was hanging on to the sleeve of my ski suit, and the other was that I'd just never been able to keep my mouth shut! "If you must know, his name is Hans."

"Hans?" He wrinkled his forehead. "I can't remember an instructor called Hans—and I thought I knew them all." His face cleared. "Anyway, you don't need an instructor, Jo; I can teach you anything you need to know."

On their own the words sounded innocent enough, but I would have had to have had all my senses impaired—no, make that be *dead*—not to catch his meaning. "You wish! Get a life, Justin, preferably one that lets you think above your jocks!"

As I stormed into the dining room, I figured that the Justins of this world would be great diet aids. Doctors could package them up and prescribe them as appetite suppressants, because one dose and they sure as heck would put you off food!

And pain relief! Because I was suddenly feeling much stronger.

Dad beamed at me when I entered the room, closely followed by Justin, but I just glared back. If he said one word, just one word . . .

The look Kate shot me was one of sympathy, but I ignored that, too. Not that I wasn't grateful, but the tears of anger that were building up in the backs of my eyes were threatening to fall. And if she was too nice to me then they might just do it.

And I would hate it if Justin thought he'd made me cry.

Hans was waiting for me at the ski lift. Relief washed through me; I didn't have to share him with a whole other class. Maybe it was the fact that school had gone back, or maybe he'd swapped classes with some of the other instructors, or maybe most of the people at the resort were seasoned skiers . . . I didn't know.

Whatever the reason, I wasn't arguing with the fact that I just about had Hans all to myself. Only one thought bothered me, and that was that if he really wasn't royal and filthy rich, I'd hate him to be sacrificing his paycheck to be with me. It was a very romantic thought, though. . . .

If my grin was too goofy he didn't comment.

On that thought I was ready for the day. Not that

it was much of a day. After my encounters with Justin and my rush to get to Hans, I hadn't really noticed the weather until now. This morning was the total opposite of the last few days: it was really bleak. The sky was this yucky gray-green color, and its reflection made everything look strange. It was much colder, too, and I was glad I'd put on just about every accessory I had—like two pairs of gloves, and a wooly cap as well as a headband!

The outfit made me feel good, too. The suit I had on was this really cool silvery color—I loved it! It had these little lines of pink and purple running through it that kind of shimmered when the sun shone on them. Pity there wasn't any sun! Add this to my wraparound sunnies and I thought I looked about as great as it was possible for me to look in one of these outsize moon suits.

I was to find out that it had been a bad choice. . . .

Hans, though, looked fabulous in a bright blue suit and white woolen cap with a huge pom-pom on the top. I couldn't see his eyes because of his giant reflector goggles. Actually, instead I could see myself really clearly in the mirrored lenses and decided to pull myself together. I looked like a lovesick cow! I straightened up.

I could be cool.

I *would* be cool.

Good intentions or not, I nearly fainted when he

leaned over and put his arms around my neck a few seconds later! It took a full minute of confusion during which I nearly hugged him back, before I realized he was simply adjusting my scarf up over my mouth. "You vill need zis; ze wind is very cold today."

I nodded, glad that between the glasses and the scarf, most of my face was covered—that way he couldn't see the extent of my embarrassment. I even started waving my arms around in front of myself, just in case he'd thought that I actually *had* been intending to hug him, that he'd realize I was just doing some warm-up exercises. At least I hoped that was what he would think. Talk about overkill.

We rounded the building with Hans urging me toward the lift. Dad had already organized my passes, so I really just had to show up and flash them and we were on our way.

I'd been so absorbed with my own thoughts that I hadn't paid any attention to the lift. Till now. "I'm not going on that! Where's the seat? Where's the seat *belt*?!" The guy was crazy if he thought that I was going to risk my life—my very *young* life—on some metal T-bar contraption that didn't even have as much as a rubber band to hold me on to it!

Hans put his arm around my waist, or at least where my waist was supposed to be in this stupid suit. "Zis is safe, Jo. I promise zat nothing vill hap-

pen to you. I vill hold your hand all ze way." He
was whispering in my ear and it was sending tingles
down through my body.

I gazed into his mirrored sunnies and decided
with a sigh that at least it would be a romantic
death.

Actually, the operation was fairly simple. The T-
bar fitted in against my backside, and once I was
sure that I could hold my poles under one arm and
grip the line in front of me with the other, I relaxed
and let the lift drag me up the slope. It helped enor-
mously that Hans's hand was on top of mine the
whole time—even if three pairs of gloves separated
our flesh.

The rest of the morning was a rage. Hans taught
me all this really neat stuff, like using my body to
turn and swerve, and sliding down little slopes
without my poles to help with control. It was really
cool, and I'm not just talking about the weather. I
should be ashamed to admit that there were a few
times when I pretended not to understand something and Hans would have to come and put his
arms around me to explain a bit better. I *should* be
ashamed, but I'm not. Sometimes a girl has to take
her future into her own hands! Besides, it was important that Hans understand what American girls
were like. You know, fun and friendly but not
pushovers. Smart. Good sports. Basically, good
future-wife material.

Good ambassadors for royal families . . .

Unfortunately, if I'd worried less about that and more about our surroundings, maybe I wouldn't have gotten such a shock a few minutes later. I supposed Hans had been keeping an eye on the weather, but to me things suddenly started to look a bit different. It was hard to tell where the sky ended and the snow started; everything was a gray-white color. Everything! Me included. My silver suit was making me blend into the scenery.

"Hans! What's happening? I can hardly see in front of me!"

"Do not panic, Jo. Zis is called a whiteout, but perhaps it vould be better if we return to the bottom."

"But how? Excuse me for seeming totally dim, but I can hardly even make out the trees, let alone the trail!"

There weren't many people just where we were, and I was starting to get really freaked. Hans was obviously used to this, but I guess it was his job to humor me.

"It vill be easy, Jo. You know how to handle your skis, so just follow ze run."

"I can't!"

Hans sounded like he was starting to lose patience. "Vell, then . . ." He seemed to be searching for something to say that would calm me down. I could have told him he had an impossible job ahead of him. "Look! See zat skier ahead, ze one in ze bright yellow?" he finally said. "Follow him. I vill be right behind you."

"Really? Promise?"

I took a deep breath. Okay. I can follow simple directions. Just trail the guy in yellow. What could be simpler than that? My heart did a huge backflip. Simpler than that? Oh, probably only the square root of 967,000 added to the sum of the product of three isosceles triangles! Cubed! In other words, it was totally *not* possible. For me, anyway.

I tossed up the options for one second flat: ski down the trail or be lost in the snow forever? I narrowed the option: ski or miss dinner. Miss every dinner from now till eternity.

I was starving.

It wasn't a choice.

I set off slowly, trying to remember everything Hans had taught me, as well as concentrating on the guy in front in yellow, who was much faster and disappearing with alarming speed. To make matters worse it had started to snow fairly hard. The guy in front was now only a yellow dot. "Oh, no! He's gone . . . disappeared!"

I swerved to a stop, spraying newly fallen snow. If I could just get another glimpse of him . . . My concentration must have been really intense, because my first realization of Hans was when he plowed straight into me and sent me flying!

I think I came off best; my last sight of Hans had been of him diving to the right to try to save himself from a worse collision with an unforgiving giant pine.

And then Hans was lying in a crumpled mess in the snow!

In the next seconds I finally fully understood the value of poles to a skier as I scrambled to my feet determined to get to my poor Hans.

He'd be so worried about me! I hoped he hadn't bumped his head. Oh, Lordy, what if he'd forgotten how to speak English? No. He'd be okay. He had to be! As I brushed the snow away from his face, I imagined his first words. I could almost hear them: *I vill be fine. Zere is nothing to vorry about . . . But my sweet, are you harmed? Is my precious bebbee hurt? Is my future princess safe?*

I was ready to swoon.

Instead his arms suddenly shot out and grabbed mine, holding me hard against him in a death grip. I looked into his face where bright blue eyes stared back at me. Angry eyes.

Angry?

That wasn't in the plan . . .

My own eyes wandered down to his mouth. *Words*, I silently encouraged. *Say the words.* "Hans?"

The eyes flashed again. "Of all the stupid, lame-brained things to do! Why in the hell did you stop?

Only a flamin' sheila would pull an airhead stunt like that!"

Imagine that.

I got the words. And all delivered with not one hint of accent.

At least, not a German one . . .

Chapter Four

I quickly regrouped to assess the situation calmly. *Sheila?* Interesting German word.

Not!

I let go of his snowsuit and eyed him through half-closed eyes. I was experiencing one of those little moments where a light goes on in your head. Except that in my case it was as bright as an entire fireworks show.

Something was going down here—and I had a feeling I knew what it was. I put my suspicions to the test.

"Ach du lieber Ziet!" I challenged him. To be honest, I wasn't even exactly sure what it meant myself. All I knew was that it was German, and that it ended in an exclamation mark, so I hoped it was bad. Actually I hoped it translated to "You are the biggest D-head in the entire universe!"

It probably didn't.

That statement delivered, I sat back as best I could on my haunches and waited with interest for his reaction.

He was still looking a bit dazed, which I figured was to my advantage at that precise moment. "What?" he asked.

I gave him one last try. This time I played it safe with a regular first-lesson German phrase. *"Guten morgen."* I watched his face closely—no lights flashed on. As a matter of fact, he was staring at me as if I were talking in a foreign language.

Which of course I was.

His foreign language. Or what was supposed to be his foreign language!

Still no response. The truth was staring me in the face. *My* German might not be very good—but it was better than Hans Gottlieb's German. Hans Gottlieb's German was nonexistent!

The heel clicking, bow-at-the-waist, Swiss ski instructor was no more Swiss than I was! He was a fake! And he didn't even realize yet that he'd just given himself away. I continued to watch him, one eyebrow raised in that way Madonna does when she's being really cool and really tough. I was not going to make this easy. But I was also not going to freeze to death! I was just about to yell at him to hurry up before my face froze in that position and I ended up with one eyebrow stuck permanently in my hairline, when it happened.

It was like a light really did come on in his eyes. One second he was looking at me like I had two heads, and the next he groaned out loud and covered his face with his hands.

"I blew it, didn't I?"

"You sure did, *mate*. Got any shrimps to throw on the barbie? Isn't that what you Australians do best? You are Australian, aren't you? Or is this another pose?" I could have chosen worse words to throw at him, but they couldn't have been delivered in a worse way. I was really making him squirm, and it felt good. One of the best parts was watching him watch me. He looked a bit like a mouse watching a cat. He didn't have a clue what I was going to do next, but he did know that he probably wasn't going to like it.

He obviously figured that he'd take his chances with an explanation. "Hey, look, Jo, I really was going to tell you. . . . Honest. It was just that I started this dumb scam and then I didn't flamin' well know how to get out of it."

Yeah, right!

Perhaps he read my disbelief in my eyes, because he went for attempt number two. "It's true, Jo! I really want to explain—"

"Save it, *mate*." To be fair, this was one story I really wanted to hear. But snow was falling harder now, and more than to hear his explanation, I wanted *not* to be lost forever in these snow-covered mountains with a guy with an identity crisis as my only companion. "You'll get your time in court. Right now I don't care if you have to pig-gyback me, just get me off this mountain! You *do* know how to get down off this mountain, don't you? After all, you *are* a long way from home."

I could still see the uncertainty in his eyes; it seemed like now that he'd been caught, he wanted to have it all out and get it over with, but I wasn't ready to give him that chance. The truth was, I didn't really know how I felt. Part of me wanted to slam him and part of me wanted to totally hoot. I mean, what a ham! What kind of a dork pretends he speaks in another language? Hello? I stopped doing that in fifth grade!

The really dumb thing was that now the phony accent was gone, he didn't even look European anymore! And not that I was ready to tell him yet, but his Aussie accent was waaay cuter than his German accent had been, anyway. And his suffer-ing was cute, too. Maybe if he suffered a bit more he'd realize more quickly that he really was madly in *lerve* with me. . . . Correction. Make that looove without the Euro accent.

Hmm . . . Yes, suffering could be good.

When he finally got to his feet and turned away to grab his poles, I swallowed back a grin. Can you fall in love with the same person twice? I guess if you think they're different people, it's okay. Or maybe I'd just performed another personal best. I don't know why I hadn't seen it before. It was right there in full view—Heath Ledger and Russell Crowe thrown into one! My cell phone would get a workout tonight. Maybe I'd borrow Dad's laptop. Hotmail, here I come!

It was a long, slow trip to the bottom. I mean, have you ever tried to ski with someone holding on to the back of your jacket? I haven't either, but it must have been hell on Aussie what's-his-name, because I practically made him drag me along the path.

The good thing was that the closer we got to the bottom, the even funnier the whole thing seemed. I was actually giggling as we undid our skis and dumped them back at the office, until this voice roared out, "Philpott! Where in the hell have you been? I've been looking everywhere to tell you that your nursery session for this afternoon is canceled."

"Sorry, boss; we were a bit slow getting back."

I didn't miss the meaningful look that was shot my way.

"Do you want me to do anything else this arvo?"

"Nah, I think we'll have to close off the main runs." The guy was obviously busy, because he didn't even say good-bye before he strode back off toward the administration office.

Not that I cared about that. By this time I was

ready to free-fall into the snow. My legs were not going to hold me up with this one! "Philpott?" I managed to gasp. "Your real name is Philpott?"

"Philpott" dropped his hands in a resigned way. "If I'm coming clean, you might as well know the rest. It gets worse. . . . My full name is *Frewin* Philpott."

That was it; there was no holding back. I laughed so hard that I cried. "Why didn't your parents just drown you at birth if they hated you so much?"

Even Frewin cracked up. "Yeah, it doesn't quite have the same ring to it as Brad Pitt or Mel Gibson, does it? Unfortunately, Frewin is a good old Philpott family name . . . I'm the fifth. The first was some whining old Scotsman."

"What made you think that *anyone* would ever believe that you were Hans Gottleib?"

"You did."

"Oh." Now, that was a sobering thought! "Only because I'm used to associating with people who've got the courage to be themselves."

"Only because you thought it'd be cool to tell your mates that you met a Swiss ski instructor, you mean! Come on, Jo! I scammed you, but you fell for it because you wanted to believe it."

He was right—we were both at fault. "Okay, we'll call this round a draw."

He seemed to relax, as though my opinion was important to him. . . . Or maybe he was just scared

I'd tell his boss. Whatever his reasons, they were rapidly becoming secondary to the fact that I was freezing. "Hey, before we find any more reasons to end this truce, could you do me one huge favor? Would you check to see if I still have a nose?"

"Aha! Something I can cure! Super Frewin to the rescue! Steaming hot chocolate—it'll have you thawed in no time."

"Only if I can bathe in it."

As we jogged along, smacking our hands together to ward off the cold, Frewin filled me in on the Hans scam. "All season I've been watching the older guys do it. They reckon it pulls the chicks, and it seems to work. Well, they've been ribbing me about having a go, and I was pretty keen to try. I didn't plan that it was going to be you. But when I dragged you out of the way of that shredder, it just sort of hit me that here I was with a cute girl and, well, why not go for it? What I didn't bet on was realizing that I'd really like you and wanting you to like *me* . . . Frew. Not Hans."

"So why didn't you just tell me?"

"Man, I didn't know how! I knew I was in trouble from the first. When you wanted to talk in German, that really spun me out!"

"You needn't have worried. No one understands my German, not even my German teacher. And most of the time she's reading what I'm supposed to be saying! As a matter of fact, I'm almost famous for it. My school got a letter from the German Embassy asking that I not be allowed to speak their language in public . . . it offended them."

"You're kidding!"

"Yeah, I am. But it's almost that bad."

"You know, you kind of did me a favor today. If you hadn't been wearing that silver-gray suit then I probably wouldn't have crashed into you. What with the whiteout and all, I didn't see you until I was almost on top of you. And if I hadn't crashed into you then I'd still be trying to find a way to tell you who I am. I'm really grateful to you, Jo."

Yeah, right. Like I'd fall for that—these Aussie guys were smooth. I had a feeling that I'd just been snowballed—pun intended—but it didn't matter; I'd forgiven him anyway.

The little coffee shop was packed, and we squeezed in against the wall. The warmth kicked in so fast I thought I was going to melt right into a puddle on the floor. Or was that just because I was squeezed in next to Frewin? *Frewin!* Man! That was going to take some getting used to . . .

People in ski suits jammed around tables called out to one another, cracking jokes and ribbing one another. Waitresses in bright red ski sweaters joined in the wisecracking as they threaded their way through tiny aisles balancing loaded trays. Man, it was like one big party!

Steam from cappuccino machines and various

pots drifted toward the dark-beamed ceiling. The mouthwatering aromas of coffee and chocolate mingled with the delicious smells of fresh-baked rolls and melted cheese. One deep breath and I swear I gained five pounds! And I didn't care. Calorie-fest, here I come! I was in heaven! I didn't even care if I was forced to stand there propped up against a wall all afternoon. I was delirious with contentment. The promise of great food, Frewin . . . What more could I want?

Some more people came in and pushed us farther along the wall—that meant Frew had to move even closer. Much closer. Like right up against me. *Oh, my! Be still, my beating heart. . . .*

I looked up into his face, and he looked like he was scanning for an empty table. But I could tell by his body language that that was just a cover; he was loving this squeezy environment as much as I was. He wanted to stay just where we were all afternoon—just like I did. . . .

We were so alike. Made for each other . . . This was so dreamy. I leaned in a bit closer . . .

And suddenly felt myself free-falling into the arms of some stranger who didn't look like he was real happy about catching me! The only thing that saved me from a nasty fate with the hardwood floor was that the guy I was aiming for couldn't move due to the crush of people behind him. What happened? "Frew?" My voice was choked, garbled.

"Jo! Over here!"

Dazed, I pulled myself up, adjusted my woolen cap back into place from where it had been pushed over one eye, and pulled my scarf out of my mouth, spitting out wool tufts as I went. And I followed his voice—halfway across the room.

"Where did you go? H-how did you get there?"

He was beaming. "I've been watching for a table! You gotta be fast in these places. It takes complete concentration—but I was ready to pounce. Here! Come and sit down."

So much for his obsession with me. . . .

Straightening myself up, I swallowed deeply and tottered across to the table, pretending all the while that everything was perfectly okay and that I hadn't just made a huge fool of myself. Again.

Hot chocolate and toast ordered, I peeled off my hat, gloves, and scarves, and forced myself to remember *I* was the one who'd been scammed, and that cute or not, the guy owed me some answers.

"Where do you really come from? How come you aren't at school? Is this a full-time job? Do they have royalty in Australia?" Had that one sounded too hopeful? And the biggie . . . "Have you got a girlfriend?"

He sat back and looked at me in awe. "Man! What is this? An inquisition?"

I was hurt. "What's wrong with asking questions?" How else was I supposed to find out about him? "It's not like I asked you anything *really* personal. . . ."

He nearly choked. "How much more personal can you get?" he asked incredulously.

I shrugged and tugged on a curl that had fallen forward. "Well, I *could* have asked for your chest measurement, or your IQ, or your father's annual income, or, er . . . if you've ever . . ."

"If I've ever *what*!?" This time he *did* choke, his eyes huge and bulging.

I had to think quickly. "If you've ever, um . . . ridden a surfboard?" I finished lamely.

"Have I ever 'um . . . ridden a surfboard'?" he repeated slowly. His eyes narrowed as if he were trying to work out if that's what I'd really been going to ask him, and I could feel myself going bright red. Finally he sighed, his eyes still fully on me.

I assumed my most innocent look—the one that always got me out of trouble in class. "What? Why are you looking at me like that? I think you should be grateful!" I answered indignantly. "After all, those are the questions I *didn't* ask you. Surely that makes it fairly easy to answer the ones that I *did* ask!"

Frewin shook his head. "I reckon it was easier being Hans!"

Our food arrived and I allowed us both a few minutes to drool over the creamiest hot chocolate I'd ever tasted before prompting him: "Well . . . ? Are you going to give?"

He lifted his hands in a gesture that told me that I'd asked for it. "Okay, but you should know that listening to my life story comes with a surgeon general's warning. It's a health hazard—people have been known to die of boredom."

I stayed silent, forcing him to continue. It worked.

He sighed again and shook his head. "I live in New South Wales. Bottom part of the state— southwest. Kind of this really tiny country town. My folks have got a small dairy farm down there. I've got three brothers and a sister and . . . jeez—I don't know; what else is there to tell?"

"Plenty! Like how come you're working here and when did you leave school?"

"I graduated senior high last year. And this is just a job."

"But where do you stay?"

"At the instructors' quarters."

"Come on, Frewin—spill! This is a pretty classy place. I can't imagine that just *anyone* could get a job here as an instructor!"

"*Junior* instructor." He seemed embarrassed, and I got the distinct impression that he was holding something back. My intuition never fails me at crucial times. For just a second I had a flash of all the goof-ups I'd made based on intuition in the past two days, but I shrugged them off. It was obviously the altitude. Once I had it mastered, I'd be back to making perfect intuitional scores again.

"And?"

He looked really uncomfortable. Good. My powers were coming back.

"Don't you ever give up? Okay, so I'm the Australian junior downhill ski champion."

He was what? Oh, man! This called for texting *and* e-mailing! "Wow!" I mean, what could I say? Like, here I was sitting with a celebrity! "Wow!" I repeated.

"Cut it out, will you? Oh, jeez. If you must know, it's not that big a deal in Australia. Snow sports aren't really huge there. Not like football and, well, swimming or surfing."

"Surfing is big?" I felt my eyes glaze over. Briefly, I romanced the idea of him carrying me back to Australia on the back of a kangaroo or something, where I'd become a citizen and go on to become Australia's female surfing champion. It was perfect! See? I knew we were meant to be together—I just hadn't made the right connection. And I'd still get a crown! The surfing crown!

"Glad you aren't that overwhelmed after all," he

added dryly—probably because I hadn't spoken for several minutes.

Oops. I hoped he wasn't a champion mind reader as well. I smiled weakly and quickly rewound the conversation back to what happened before he mentioned surfing. "No! Hey, I'm really impressed. How did you get to be so good?"

He grinned. "It's okay. It's really not that big of a deal."

Oh, man. I had some major making up to do. "It really is. Do you live in the snow country or what? Actually I gotta admit I didn't know Australia even had any snow. I thought it was just really hot down there." Again I flashed the dimples and hoped to dazzle him. It must have worked, because he sighed and shook his head.

"It's pretty hot and dry where I live. Gets cold in winter but not cold enough to snow. And if it did, it wouldn't be enough to ski on. But I've got an uncle who lives near the slopes in Victoria. Ever since I was a little kid he's been taking us skiing, and . . . well, I guess I just had a knack or something."

I laughed. "A knack? You call being a national champion 'a knack'?" Oh, Lordy—this guy was too cute for words. And that accent!

"Well, practice helped. My uncle made sure I got to ski as much as possible every season and started entering me in local comps. I reckon it was a fluke that I won the big one, but I'm not complaining. It got me a job here."

"But . . . is this all you want to do? Teach skiing?"

"Nah . . ." He paused. "You'll probably think I'm really dorky, but I want to have a stab at the winter Olympics."

"Really? No! I don't think that's dorky—I think it's really cool!" Oh, man—even to my own ears I sounded like a gushing idiot, but the guy had blown me away. I was in *looove* with a future world champion—a future gold medalist! Oh, man! His face would be plastered on billboards everywhere. Like, he'd be advertising some soda, or maybe sportswear. Oh, no! The *National Enquirer* would follow us everywhere. We'd be hounded by paparazzi! I pushed away the rest of my hot chocolate. I simply could not afford to gain one ounce! Photos add ten pounds! I had to be ready! Had to go into celeb photo training!

"Are you okay?" he asked. "You're looking kinda dazed. Is your chocolate okay?"

"Me?" I squeaked, as I dragged back the offending mug. "I'm fine! Wonderful! It's just that I've never met a champion anything before. Hang on; that's not quite true—but I don't think that Lenny Birkowitz is quite in your category. He's the local soft-candy-eating champ. That includes unwrapping time. Five pounds in ten minutes in case you're . . . I mean, I thought you might . . . be . . . interested." I paused and cleared my throat. "Okay. I'm shutting right up now."

I'd proved it; I was a fool, a blubbering, brainless fool! Why would a national ski champion be interested in hearing about an overweight foodaholic? I moved the mug away again and folded the paper napkin three different ways. Now I'd never make the pages of the *National Enquirer* . . . Unless it was in the "Girlfriends I am glad I dumped" column. Oh, jeez! And I wasn't even his girlfriend yet! And I was getting dumped!

From the other side of the table after a seemingly endless silence I heard, "Vell, Jo, I can see zat you attract ze people vis ze hidden talents. . . ."

I chanced a glance upward and found him trying hard to keep a straight face. Almost against my will I found myself laughing, too. "Believe me, there's nothing 'hidden' about the effects of Lenny's talents! He's, like, two hundred and fifty pounds!" I was really grateful to Frewin just then—I'd been making a such a huge fool of myself, but he'd brought us back on track. Frewin Philpott was a nice guy. I could even live with his name. Weird as it was, I was actually starting to like the name Frewin. . . . It kind of suited him. Frewin Philpott. What was it with me? I swear my mind was totally out of control, because I could not make it stop taking it that one step further:

Frew Philpott. Jo Philpott?

Jo Philpott: Australian women's surfing champion—and wife of gold medalist world champion downhill skier Frewin Philpott.

I sighed. It had a nice, simple ring to it.

"So," I went on, recovering quickly, "how do you go about getting to the Olympics?"

"Well, actually that's the real reason I'm here. You see, to have any kind of chance I have to get as much practice as I can. That's a bit hard in a country that only has about two months of really good snow a year. Over here in the States and in Europe they have these neat ski compounds—and I'm trying for a scholarship for one. Or some sponsorship. My folks haven't got the kind of money I need to pay my way, so I'm working here and trying to attract a sponsor. If I can pull it off then I reckon I've got at least a bit of a chance. If not, then it's back to school or the farm."

I put my hand up in a high-five sign. "I really hope you make it." And I meant it.

His hand met mine, but instead of the usual smack, he held on and we stayed like that for a second.

"And Jo? Just for the record, mate, I haven't got a girlfriend and I haven't, um . . . er, ridden a surfboard, if you know what I mean."

His eyes locked with mine for a moment while I took in his message. I felt myself flush. I must have looked like Rudolph the Red-Nosed Reindeer with a leak. "Um . . . me either."

Chapter Five

It was breakfast on day three, and Dad was having one of his rare conversations with me. Cool. It helped that I was feeling pretty great, due to the fact that my friends back in California were just sooo jealous. They could not believe I had my own Heath Ledger/Russell Crowe–combination clone. All I needed was for him to wrestle a crocodile for me and I bet I'd be the envy of the entire female population of my whole school. Maybe my whole town. Maybe my whole state! I'd probably be voted best something or other. Maybe "best hot-guy magnet!"

I'd hardly been able to sleep last night. My friends didn't help 'cause they just kept texting with so many questions. They wanted to know simply *everything*. I was their hero! This was the coolest vacation ever, and even if I hated to admit it, Dad was the one responsible for it.

"So have you learned to stay upright yet, Josephine?" Dad continued.

"Kind of. I do know I'm really starting to take to this snow life. Skiing is pretty wild. A bit like surfing in a way. I can see why some kids love both. Maybe you could see for yourself how I'm doing later? I booked Hot Shotz to do one of those half-hour videos. You know the ones? You take them home and bore your friends with the vacation shots . . . proof-that-you-really-were-there kind of thing."

I finished on a laugh—but no one joined in.

In fact, silence was all that greeted me, and I was suddenly and painfully wrenched out of my fantasy world and back into reality. My face burned. That had been a dumb thing to say. I think I was just caught up in the fact that my dad was actually talking to me and not yelling and not ordering. Hello? Reality check: Why would my father want to watch a video of *me*?

His next words proved that he probably hadn't heard a word I'd said anyway. He made no mention of the video, and I didn't know whether to be justified in that I really knew how he felt, or just burst into tears there and then! However, once the words sank in, they soon shoved away any tears— at least any sad ones.

"Justin tells me that you're being instructed by someone called Hans."

I opened my mouth to explain that Hans was really Frewin, but out of the corner of my eye I could see that sleazy Justin was hanging on every word I said, and somehow it seemed unfair to Frewin to talk about it in front of him. I could imagine that Justin would really enjoy bringing Frew down, so I figured it was a story for another time, and played along. Even if I *was* privately ticked off that Dad could barely focus on one conversation with me and yet he remembered every word Justin uttered. "Yeah, he's really cool. He's a really great skier, Dad. It's his day off today and he's taking me up to Ranger's Peak and I think we're going to have lunch at the restaurant. It's supposed to be really great up there."

Obviously I'd made mistake number one. I caught the frown that crossed Dad's face and prepared myself for the worst, trying to angle myself away from Justin's prying eyes.

"You aren't getting too friendly with this instructor, are you, Josephine? These people are like vagabonds; they just follow the snow season from place to place. They're not responsible, not building futures. . . . Some of them even have reputations for being lowlifes!"

I shook my head at him, pushing back the anger that threatened to boil over and scald us all. "Give it a break, Dad! You're such a snob! And anyway, Fr—I mean Hans isn't like that! He's got big plans. He—"

"Josephine, I really would rather you spend the day with Justin. I'm sure he wouldn't mind showing you around."

Justin leered. My skin crawled.

"Come on, Dad. You know nothing about this guy! Give him a break! I'll be okay, truly. If you'll just let me expl—"

"No, Josephine, it's settled. You're a very eligible young woman, you know! People can take advantage! I'll feel much better knowing that you're going to be with someone responsible."

Justin leaned back in his seat out of Dad's line of vision and grinned at me like a dieter who'd just discovered a secret stash of Hershey bars.

It took every ounce of willpower not to give him the bird right there and then. My father knew nothing about so-called lowlifes! The biggest one was sitting right there at that very table with him. Trouble was, if I tried to tell him, he'd just say I was being difficult—or that it was my imagination! Personally, right then I would rather have taken my chances with a sex-starved football team.

The breakfast I'd just eaten agreed with my feelings of repugnance, because I could feel it start its upward journey. Like me, it wanted out!

"Ah, excuse me; I suddenly don't feel well. . . . I'd like to go back to my room."

I heard Dad's sigh and ignored it. Actually I started to feel much better as soon as I was out of Justin's sight. There was no way I was spending the day with him, so I sprinted up the stairs to grab the rest of my gear with the aim of being out the door before he even knew I'd gone.

But even the greatest plans have their flaws. And the one in this plan was that Justin had figured that I'd try to make the bolt and was waiting for me at the door. I almost skidded into him in my attempt to get free.

"Really keen to spend the day with me, eh, babe?"

His breath washed over me and sent me reeling. Hadn't the guy heard of a toothbrush and tooth-paste? "In your dreams, Justin. The only thing I'm keen for is for you to get out of my face. And to find a respirator! Get some mouthwash!"

His eyes narrowed. He hadn't liked the barb. Who cared? "Ooooh. Daddy's not going to be pleased. He seems to think that we'd be good to-gether. And me? I, for one, know we'd be real *good*. I know I can make it real good. . . ."

My stomach churned again. "Fortunately I'm not responsible for my father's delusions. So take a hike, would you?"

His answer was to put his arm around me and

pull me in tight. He whispered, "You know, Josephine, most little high school chicks like you would die for the chance to boast to their friends that they've been with a college man—here's your chance."

I tried to push away with all my strength, wishing that the bulk of my ski suit hadn't made using my knee a bit awkward. "You're sick, Justin—why don't you just crawl back under your rock? I can't imagine any female in the entire universe would want to do anything with you except crush you under her boot. And as for your college education, I'd chuck it in, pal. The way I see it, the only talent you've got is obvious, and I don't think they've got a degree course in sleazeball!"

Justin shrugged as if he suddenly couldn't care less. He let me go so fast I had to grab the wall to save myself from head-butting the carpet. The guy was totally weird. His brain cells were too fried to make any sense. "It's your loss, babe. See you around. But," he added as he turned to walk away, "if I see *Daddy* I'll have to tell him the truth: that you're off chasing Hans around the snowfields."

I closed my eyes to count to ten. The guy was like a disease! Eeeeooww! Yuk!

I didn't even see where he'd disappeared to—maybe back to his cave. When I opened my eyes again he was gone, and that was all I cared about. That was all the encouragement I needed to put as much space between him and me as possible.

The freezing air felt great after that showdown. Kind of cleansing. More than ever I wanted to find Frew, to kid around with him, to laugh with him and listen to his dumb jokes. . . . To just be with someone normal . . .

I found him standing near this little copse of fir trees on the way to the main village. There wasn't much else around on this part of the trail, so we had the place to ourselves.

His grin reached out to me from ten feet away.

"Gidday! What's up? You look like you've found out that the United Nations has banned tomato sauce! Ketchup to you," he added with a grin.

"Worse," I muttered.

Frewin shook his head, his face suddenly a portrait of misery. "Believe me, nothing—and I mean *nothing*—could be as bad as a world without tomato sauce—er, ketchup. Especially if your mum is as bad a cook as mine is . . ." He put his hands around his own neck as if he were choking, and I started to chuckle. That Russell Crowe voice was doing its stuff; I could feel my mood lifting.

"In that case, I don't suppose my problem *is* as bad as yours."

Frew didn't answer; he just waited, staring at me. Those eyes! They just kind of speared a girl. . . . I threw my hands in the air. "Look, I'm okay. Really! I was just thinking about something, but it'll pass. So if you're waiting for any other explanation . . ." I shrugged; I didn't want to talk about Justin. I just wanted to forget he existed.

"Not good enough. Come on, this is a holiday. You gotta loosen up. . . ."

His voice was suddenly weird. Suspicion rippled down my spine. "What's going on?"

He was moving backward away from me. Why hadn't I noticed his hands had stayed behind his back this whole time? Reality dawned. He wouldn't! He couldn't!

He did!

It was a perfect shot.

"Ouch! What the . . . ? You rat! Ouch! What are you doing?" Stupid question! It was *obvious* what he was doing. He'd just caught me unprepared for the barrage of snowballs that were being mercilessly hurled at me. But I'm a fast learner. "Right—you want war? Then war you'll get! I'm just in the right mood!"

I'd never made a snowball and didn't realize that there was an art to it. The balls that I was throwing were soft and mushy and didn't have much impact—much to Frew's enjoyment. It didn't take me long to realize that he was throwing faster than I could make them. Actually when I thought about it, he was throwing them faster than *he* could *make* them. What was the deal here?

Pretending to crouch down I watched as he

slipped behind a small bush. Aha! I'd found his arsenal. Now I just had to lure him away and capture it.

I started to steadily circle, arcing my way closer. I kept ducking from his bombs, taking shelter in the trees, trying all the while to land a few of my own. I waited for the moment. It came. He slipped in behind the shrubbery that held his stash, and I ran and hid behind a huge tree just a few feet or so away. I waited for him to realize that I wasn't in sight.

"Jo-oo . . . where are you?" He was calling in that singsong voice kids have used for centuries to trick their friends out of hiding. "Come on out . . . I'm empty-handed . . . I promise. . . ."

Yeah, right! As if I'd fall for that! I pushed my face into my sleeve to stop from cracking up. This was wild. The adrenaline was really pumping through my body. I sensed when his voice moved farther away; now was the moment. I peeked out carefully. Frew was about ten feet away with his back to me.

As silently as I could, I dived in behind his secret shrubbery hideout, executing a perfect commando roll as I fell into place. I'd made it! Double-oh-seven, eat your heart out! Quickly I took in my surroundings—and a grin spread all over my face at the sight before me. The rat! The dirty rat! This was no impromptu snow fight! The huge pile of snowballs all ready and waiting was solid proof. . . .

This was a planned attack! An ambush! Ha!

I waited again, sure he could hear my heartbeat, not so sure I could stifle my own giggles.

It happened. I heard him turn, his voice coming back in my direction. I could even hear his boots crunch on the snow as he got closer. I tried to work out just how close he was. I had to take my chance. . . . Two, three . . . Now!

"Take that, Philpott! And that and that!" I jumped up from behind my cover and was really firing—literally! Poor old Frew let go with the couple of missiles he had left, but he was exactly where I wanted him—at my mercy.

He'd turned his back, but he couldn't escape my aim. "You can run, but you can't hide, my friend!" I let go with another. "That's for planning this attack." And another: "That's for the unfair advantage." And another: "That's for—"

"I surrender! I surrender! You win! No more!"

"Ha! Typical of a guy! Can't take the heat, huh?" I stopped midswing, ready to make him beg for my mercy, loving that heady feeling of superiority. "I'll think about it—depends on how well you grovel," I told him as I watched him edge his way warily toward me.

I learned two things in the next few minutes. One was never to trust a guy, even one waving a white flag. Second, and more important, I learned just how much I liked Frewin Philpott.

I was totally unprepared for the dive. One minute I was wondering whether to play dirty and blast him with one last shot, and the next I was the object of a waist-high tackle that sent me backward onto a soft cushion of snow, pinned by Frewin's thighs and arms.

"Now, my lovely," Frewin began in his best villain imitation, "what was that you were saying, hmmm?"

"Um," I answered, "I think I was saying that you were the best-ever snow fighter and that never again would I challenge your title."

"Chicken." The villain leered. "Unfortunately it's not good enough. To be set free you must not only grovel, but you must praise the snowball champion and you must also pay the price of surrender."

"Oh, mighty snowball champion," I went on in mock fear, "you are the fastest, the most devious, and the coolest of all snowball champions."

"Hmmm, that fulfills the second rule—and now for the third. Are you ready to pay the price of freedom?"

I'd sensed a change in Frewin; there was a seriousness about him, and a kind of stillness. I licked my lips, "Um . . . what's the price?"

"A kiss." I heard the word just seconds before his mouth came down on mine. I think that my heart actually stopped beating for a second. This had to be both the coolest and the sweetest thing that had ever happened to me.

Too soon, for me at least, it was over, but Frewin didn't let me go straightaway. Instead he stayed looking so deeply into my eyes that I thought he'd be able to see everything inside me shaking. But I wasn't the only one shaken. When at last he spoke, I knew I'd never forget his first word.

His only word . . . "Wow!"

It was poetry.

It was going to be a hot, hot Hotmail night tonight. . . . The lines would be sizzling.

"What do we do now?" Someone said that. I knew that my lips had done the work but it sure didn't sound like my voice.

"Well, to be honest, I'm feeling pretty hot right now, but we *are* lying in freezing snow." He sighed. "Maybe we should go burn some energy. I don't want your dad coming after me with a shotgun!"

The mention of my father was enough to pour cold water over any flames that might have been burning within. I'd gone past being angry with him for not wanting me to spend time with Frew; now I was kind of sad. I sat up, lost in my own thoughts for a moment.

"Jo?" Frew's voice, sort of unsure, broke into

those thoughts. "Hey, you're not upset, are you? I mean, maybe I shouldn't have—"

I smiled at him. "Nah, everything's cool. I was thinking of something else." He was looking so worried that I wanted to try to cheer him up. "Hey, have you ever made snow angels?"

"Snow what?"

"Angels. You know, they always make them in the movies. You lie down in the snow on your back, and you wave your arms and legs up and down in the snow and it makes the outline of angel's wings. I've always wanted to do it. I dare you to do it with me!" He took the dare, like I knew he would. (Males act so predictably when they think a woman can do something that they can't!)

We must have looked a scream, but it was kind of fun. There was probably no need to mention to my friends later that night that the female of this duo made the best angel. But of course I would!

Defeated, Frewin finally pulled me to my feet. "Come on. I'm starving."

For the rest of the day I think I just floated. I figured that after we'd eaten our lunch of hamburgers and the inevitable hot chocolate on top of the mountain I could nearly have floated all the way back down. As it was, I did my best skiing that day, probably because I just let my body go. And the reason for that was that although my mind was certainly on my instructor, it wasn't only his talent as a skier that had my attention.

Still, if there was a good day to get my video done it was definitely today. I was about as good as I was likely to get. I briefly wondered if I'd look attention-deficit in the video. We could call it *Snow Bunnies in Space*. What a hoot!

That was the pattern of my day. I guess my attention was somewhere else also, when Frew and I were walking along hand in hand through the boutiques later that day. Even the gorgeous hand-knitted sweaters and fabulous leather and suede gear didn't seem to penetrate. I was totally out of it. All I could seem to focus on was Frew. Face it— I'd been off the ground for so long that I almost qualified for frequent flier points!

"Hello, Josephine! Josephine?"

Frew nudged me. "Jo, I think that old bird over there is talking to you."

I turned with a start to come face-to-face with Mrs. Woods. You know, now that I looked closely at her, she seemed pretty harmless. Anyone would find it hard to believe that she was a dangerous public enemy, that she was 50 percent responsible for inflicting slimeball Justin onto this poor unsuspecting world.

She looked the part of the rich businessman's wife, though. She was loaded down with packages and was dressed in this fabulous full-length fur coat. I tried not to think about how many animals had been sacrificed so that she could stay warm. I quickly revised what I'd thought about her not looking like a public enemy.

"Oh, hi, Mrs. Woods. Sorry I didn't see you. Um, this is my friend Frewin Philpott. Frewin, Mrs. Woods and her family are staying at the lodge."

From under all those parcels she somehow managed to extend a hand. As Frew stretched his own out to grasp hers he exclaimed, "Man! Look at those rocks!"

"Frew!" My dad would have killed me for making a social clanger like that.

But Mrs. Woods just laughed. "It's all right, Josephine. This little bracelet always evokes a reaction like that." She lifted her wrist and jangled these huge stones that looked like . . .

"Diamonds! They're not really diamonds, are they? Man, they are totally wicked!" I could see why Frew had been so thrown by the sight of them. They were gorgeous. And huge! I could name islands that housed whole nations that were smaller than these stones! Well, at least I would have been able to name them if I ever paid attention in Geography.

"Of course they're diamonds, dear," she answered in a voice that was amazed that I even suspected that they were anything *but* diamonds.

" 'Struth! They must be worth a fortune!" Frew added with a frown.

To say we were a just a bit gobsmacked was a gross understatement. I guess you had to see this thing to believe it. "Aren't you scared you'll lose it? I mean, just walking around with it on. Anything could happen to it." Lordy—if I owned something like that I think I'd have it stapled onto my flesh. At least!

She waved her arm in the air, and the noise of the jangling almost caused a snowslide. "What's the good of having it if you can't wear it?" Mrs. Woods laughed. "Besides, it's insured."

She was still laughing as she walked away and it occurred to me that this was the only time I'd ever seen her look anything but bored. Obviously Mrs. Woods's enjoyment of life was measured by the limit of her credit card.

"Do you believe that?" Frew was saying. "I reckon she could feed a third-world nation for a year with just one of those rocks."

"Yeah, and have enough to spare to train ten Olympic ski champions," I added thoughtfully. Life definitely is a bitch, sometimes.

We'd made our way to yet another coffee shop, only this time I ordered coffee made with skim milk—and no food. It was part of my fight back. I figured after all that hot chocolate the fat cells on my thighs were so busy that I could almost hear them multiplying. Besides, I still had that notion *in the back of my head* of being stalked by *National Enquirer* paparazzi. And after that little smooch on the snow, could anyone blame me?

Frew was stirring his hot chocolate. Yes, more hot chocolate! Why is it that guys can eat anything? Once I got over my little internal gender-unfairness tirade, I took another look. Frew might be able to eat or drink anything he wanted, but I was pretty sure that chocolate didn't need as half as much concentration as he was giving it.

"Frew? What's up?"

"You know, I was just thinking, I never got around to asking you if you had a boyfriend."

I pursed my lips. "I should be hurt. Do you really think I'd be here with you if I did?"

He shrugged. "Get real, Jo. Heaps of chicks do. And guys do it too. I mean, you're only here on holiday, right? Sometimes it's like a bit of a holiday from their girlfriend or boyfriend, too. And then the holiday's over, and—"

"Hey, Einstein, before you wear that brain out trying to work out the world's love problems, the answer is a simple no. No, I don't have a boyfriend."

"Have you had many boyfriends? Like, are you really popular?"

I rolled my eyes. "Me, hot? Believe it, buddy! I'm the hottest thing at Franklin Vine High. I'm sizzlin'.

They're lined up. My diary is full till next fall. People vote for me on the Internet! It is definitely take-a-number time at *Casa* Jo." I sighed and let my shoulders drop in my best *I-can't-believe-you-asked-such-a-dumb-question* roll. "Jeez! What do you think?"

He grinned. What is it about cheeky Aussie grins? "I dunno—maybe I reckon it could be true. . . ."

I grinned back. "This is payback for the inquisition yesterday, isn't it?" I shook my head. "Okay, I guess I owe you some answers after what I put you through. So: Yes, I've had a few boyfriends. Not exactly heaps, and no, I'm not considered to be the hottest thing at Franklin Vine High. Although," I added just so he didn't think I was unworthy of his attention, "that could change at any time, of course. . . ."

He laughed and then quickly sobered. "Yet you've never, ah . . . ?"

"Gone all the way?"

In answer, his eyebrows went up, but he didn't say any words. But I knew that's what he'd been asking.

"Nah, none of those jerks were worth it." I made light of my answer; after all, how did you tell a guy that you were scared stiff that if your dad found out you'd done something dumb, then that'd be one more reason for him not to love you . . . ?

As if he read some of my thoughts, he asked, "How come your mum didn't come down here with you?"

I just loved the way he said *mum*. I could listen to the guy all day.

"Mom? She and Dad are divorced. Three years ago, now. This little vacation is supposed to be my 'quality time' with my father. Isn't that what they call it? That excuse they use for never having any proper time for you?"

"That's tough. You sound pretty cut up about it."

"Actually I'm just realizing that maybe it's time I started not worrying so much about what he thinks. I don't think he worries much about what *I* think."

He put his hand over mine where it lay on the table. "I reckon he thinks you're great. Don't let it get to you, mate."

Some tears welled but I swallowed them back before they made a fool of me. "Th-thanks. But you don't know my dad." I gathered our stuff. "And speaking of him, I think maybe I'd better get back." I shot him the warmest smile I could muster. "Frew? I've had the absolute best day."

His answer was a wink. "You're welcome, mate. So've I. Are we still on for tonight?"

I smiled, wondering if my heart was hanging out on my sweater like some goofy pink pulsating ball. "You bet."

Chapter Six

Back at the Chalet, I'd snatched a snack from the kitchen instead of bothering with the whole formal dinner thing. Part of it was so I could meet Frew and not be late—but there were some other good reasons for making that decision as well. Avoiding Dad and Justin topped the list. And maybe cutting back on calories by just grabbing some soup and salad didn't hurt either. All that stuff Mom went on about must have been sinking in. . . .

As I got ready to leave, I figured they'd all be going into dinner and was surprised by Dad's voice. He stood in the foyer watching me come down the stairs.

He didn't look happy. Sheesh! What was new?

"Josephine, I hear you didn't follow my suggestion today and stay with Justin. I want the truth, young lady: Did you spend the day with this Hans character?"

I looked Dad straight in the eye and told the truth. "No, Dad, I did not spend the day with Hans. I was with my friend Frewin. Ask Mrs. Woods."

"Frewin who? Where is he from? Does he have family here?"

Was this really my father speaking? Surely this must be a windup dummy or someone imitating him! Was the man who'd ignored me for three whole years really asking questions about my life for the second time in one day?

I couldn't keep the sarcasm out of my voice. "Way to go, Dad! Don't tell me—you've been taking father lessons, right? That has to be it. I can't see any other reason for all this sudden interest in my life."

He frowned. "What are you talking about? I've always been interested in you!"

I had to hand it to the guy: he was a really good actor. He almost had me believing that he was puzzled by my accusation.

"Look, Dad, I'd really love to stop and chat about this newfound interest, but Frew is waiting to meet me. And before you go rushing off to check the social register, his name is Philpott. And his family are poor Australian dairy farmers." I stopped for a second to lay my forearm against my brow. "And yes, I've decided to lower myself to his social level. Oh, the shame! Can you just see me getting scratched off college A lists as we speak!? Oh, no— no more A-list contacts!" Now I was so angry I could hardly breathe. "That's really all you wanted to know, isn't it? Sorry, Dad, but I don't think I just made another business contact for you."

My father looked ready to explode. Good—we'd make a competition out of it. "Josephine, if you think you're going to get away with th—"

"Mal . . ." Kate had appeared from almost no-where; I think she must have been curled up in one of the huge armchairs near the fire. Man, I wished I had as much influence with him as she did. Almost as soon as she spoke he stopped yelling at me and just kind of sighed, like he was really tired or some-thing. I was in awe. How did she do that? Then again, all of his girlfriends—and there were enough to warrant the description *all*—had had more influence over him than me. I shuddered, not even wanting to think about what kind of hold they'd had over him. . . . Eeooww.

The only difference with Kate was that she used her power for good instead of evil. She actually took *my* side. Amazing.

Kate the white witch moved closer to me and put her arm around my shoulders. I felt myself stiffen. It would take more than dragging my father off me to shake my mood at the moment.

"Believe it or not, he's just being a dad," she said softly.

I started to protest that it was a bit late for that, but she cut me off.

"I know, I know. . . . But you know, it might be easier if we all got together. Perhaps if we met this friend of yours? You could introduce us and then that might put your dad's mind at rest. How about lunch tomorrow?"

The lump in my throat burned. My eyes darted to my father, who still stood staring at me like he barely knew me. *Well, you got that bit right, Dad! You* do *hardly know me!* And that thought killed my anger.

Suddenly it all just seemed too hard.

Kate's hand was still warm on my shoulder and I felt some of the tension start to ease. Kate's plan was a good one. I had nothing against their meeting Frew; in fact, deep down I'd really like Dad to meet him. But unless I wanted to spill everything about his real identity right now—which I didn't think would be in the best interests of my safety—I had a bit of a problem. Frew would be working all day tomorrow!

Feeling like I was surrendering to the enemy camp, I sighed. "Tomorrow lunch? Um, that might not be that easy. You know what these skiers are like—they're worse than us surfers. Every second has to be spent on the slopes." I chewed my lip, hoping they'd buy it.

"Well, that's okay; how about dinner?"

I looked over at Dad again. He seemed quite happy to let Kate make all the arrangements, and my heart sank. Maybe his little show of interest was already fading.

"Yeah, that should be okay," I answered, wishing I didn't feel guilty about not giving them the whole story about Frew, alias Hans. Man, I knew kids who'd never been straight with their folks once in their entire lives, but that'd never really been my style, probably because Mom was so cool about everything. I made myself a promise right then that after tonight I'd tell them the whole story.

Basically I guess I'm a coward, and I was quick to work out that there was still the chance that after I'd leveled with Dad he might need some time to get used to the idea. And that could mean Dad could ground me during the process. And there was no way I was going to risk blowing this night out with Frew.

Tomorrow was another day, as they say. A much better day to come clean.

Having worked it out, I almost laughed out loud when I realized what I'd been thinking. Even if Dad *had* listened to the story he probably wouldn't give a damn anyway. The proof was here in front of me—we hadn't even finished our conversation and already he'd walked away. He was back near the fire with his head in one of those blasted magazines. He couldn't care less. What was it about me that made me so boring where he was concerned?

I looked up to see Kate watching me watch my dad. She squeezed my shoulder as if to say that everything would be okay. What a major joke!

"I'd better go." My voice was just a whisper, not because I was telling a secret, but because for a second I barely had the energy to speak. Kate nodded and let her arm drop.

But at least no one ordered me back to my room.

Frew was waiting for me at the bottom of the steps to the Chalet. He'd given me this really weird look when I'd asked him to meet me here and not inside, but I'd just brushed him off with some stupid story. I knew he didn't believe me, and I knew he'd guessed it had everything to do with my dad, but he didn't push it.

He flung his arm around my shoulder. "Gidday. Miss me?"

That accent! That grin! Suddenly all the bad things seemed to close away with the slamming door behind me. The guy was special. "Where are we going?"

"Down to one of the bars—they've got this great band playing tonight."

"But we're underage."

"It's okay. There's this underage section. It's not

the bar that's against the law to us, but what people do in it. This section is cordoned off and there's no alcohol past that point—but you still get to hear the band and stuff. But hey, if it really bugs you then we won't. We'll just go and find another coffee shop."

"Can we get into trouble if we go to a bar?"

"No, it's a legal part of the complex. It's where all the other kids here hang out. We just make sure we don't sneak any booze in and it's all okay. I'm not going to let you drink booze, Jo. That's not what this is about. And I reckon I'm not hero enough to face your dad if I took you somewhere illegal. Besides, I'm a soft-drink guy from way back."

"Soft drinks?"

He grinned. "Sodas and juice to you, Miss USA." He cracked up as he added, "And call me a wimp, but it's a bit chilly to be making out under a snow-drift. Even for us supertough Aussie guys."

I punched him in the shoulder. "Idiot! Ha! And here I thought you guys liked to live dangerously— like wrestling crocodiles and chasing deadly reptiles. Oh, well." I sighed, pretending regret. "It looks like it'll have to be the bar. . . ."

"Hey, it's no sweat to me if we don't go. You're not going to get any pressure from me—about anything."

I squeezed his hand a bit tighter. "Thanks. But

no, it's absolutely my decision—let's go. Besides, I'm a bit coffee'd out."

Like all the other buildings in the resort, the bar was warm and crowded with people. Most of the crowd were really young. Well, older than Frew and me, but not like Dad's age or anything. We found a table in the cordoned-off part, and Frew was right: most of the people around us were our age. In school vacation times it must be a blast!

In the other section there was a bit of fist banging and good-natured yelling going on, and from what we could make out the band hadn't turned up and the natives were getting restless.

The managers had started up the karaoke machine and some guy was murdering a Chili Peppers song, which had caused the crowd to turn positively ugly. It was an absolute crackup. So were the two guys who suddenly appeared in front of us bobbing up and down like marionette puppets!

"Hans!" yelled one of them over the din. "You have not introduced us to zis beautiful lady. I am Kurt and zis is Pierre."

The one doing all the talking actually bent down to kiss my hand. Over his head Frewin mouthed two words.

I nodded and when Kurt lifted his head I answered in my best French accent, " 'Allo, I am very much pleased to meet you. My name is Yvette. I am on 'oliday here from Paree! 'Ow wonderful to meet a fellow countryman!" I squealed.

Kurt's eyes immediately flew to Pierre, supposedly *French* Pierre, who looked momentarily terrified. Poor old Pierre—I guess he'd describe himself as one of life's victims. I turned on him with a rapid fire of French-sounding gobbledygook that was liberally sprinkled with lots of *"wee-wees"* (I failed French too!) and "Ooh la las." The guy froze. Well, not completely, but his face did turn a very unattractive shade of green. . . .

"You know," I went on in my Miss Paris routine, "if I 'ad to guess your names, I would never 'ave picked you to be Kurt or Pierre. Some'ow, to me you seem so much more like . . . ooh . . . maybe a Graham, and you?" I turned to poor Pierre. "Maybe a Rob?" I allowed them only a moment of stunned silence before I leaned over and whispered, "Gotcha!"

Graham, the loud one, recovered first. He turned on Frew, pretending to punch him on the shoulder. "Thanks a lot, *mate*!"

"Maybe I shouldn't have let you in on their scam," Frew said, turning to me. "I've got to room with these Romeos. Now they're likely to hang me out the window by my jocks or something!" He didn't look too worried, though.

And it was obvious by the way they laid into each other both physically and verbally that they were all good friends, even though the other two were a fair bit older than Frew. They seemed quite happy to spend the night with us, grabbing our juices and Cokes from the bar and generally hamming around. We'd taken over the jukebox, and it was during our rather painful rendition of the Doors' classic hit "People Are Strange" that our night— well, actually *my* night—started to go wrong.

I'd been having the best time of my life when suddenly someone grabbed me from behind. He—I knew it was a he—slobbered, "Hey, it's the little chick! Come and have a drink with me."

Justin! "I don't drink."

I don't usually need anyone to fight my battles either, and it wasn't as if Justin were being anything but his repulsive self, but my three companions jumped in anyway. Before I knew it they were telling him to push off. As I said, I didn't need the help—but oh, what a feeling! Imagine three hunky guys all defending little ol' me. It was nearly enough for me to denounce feminism!

I wasn't quite as delighted later, though, when all three decided to walk me home. I was kind of looking forward to being alone with Frew, and I'd have had to be blind and senseless not to pick up similar vibes from him. But the guys had other ideas. I'd have laid a bet they were paying him back for killing their scam earlier. This was not the romantic evening I'd imagined. But it had been major fun—and it was certainly one I'd remember for the rest of my life.

As I rushed up to my room and snatched up my cell phone, I wondered about my phone bill when I got back home. All this texting was gonna put me in debt to my allowance for the next three months! But did I care? It was worth every cent.

Cassie—you're not gonna believe what happened 2nite. A bar and 3 guys. Read it and weep! My texting fingers were flying. It was going be a long night. . . .

The next morning for the first time since we'd arrived I slept in. The long night of making my friends green with envy had exceeded even my expectations. I think the last message had come in at about 3:10 A.M. But after only a few minutes downstairs I'd wished I hadn't woken up at all.

"Josephine! You have some explaining to do!"

I'd been on my way to the kitchen to con some coffee and a roll out of the chef when Dad's order shook loose some of the cobwebs.

"Yeah?" I answered, wandering over to him. As usual there was no one else around; they were all either out on the slopes or trying for bankruptcy in the shops. Even the ever-present Kate seemed to be missing in action.

"Just where did you get to last night?"

"Come on, Dad, if you're this hung up about it you must know the answer."

"All right, if you're going to play smart I'll tell you what I know. You were seen at a bar! Not only that, but you were cavorting with *three* skiing instructors! May I remind you that you are only sixteen!"

"Dad, I didn't do anything wrong! It's a legal part of the bar for underage people. Ask the management! You were the one who chose this place." I sighed and tried to calm down, answering in a slow, methodical way: "Dad, listen to me. I didn't drink alcohol and I didn't approach the bar. All I did was drink soda and juice and listen to some music."

"With *three* strange men!"

"No, Dad! *Not* three strange men. With Frewin and two of his friends. Tell your informer to get his facts straight."

"I'll have you know that Justin has been very helpful!"

"I bet he has. Did he tell you that my three undesirable men friends rescued me from *him* last night as well?"

"Don't try to shift the blame, Josephine. Justin has done you a favor."

"This I've got to hear."

"Because of his concern for you, Justin has done some checking." Dad paused, and I felt like organizing a drumroll. "According to the management there is no instructor named Hans."

The last bit had come out with this huge whoosh of air, as though he'd just delivered a death warrant—or announced that McDonald's was bankrupt.

I rolled my eyes and pretended to yawn. "Oh, gee, Dad. Justin didn't have to go to all that trouble. . . . All he had to do was ask me."

I'm glad Dad's heart was in good shape; otherwise I'd have been practicing my first aid right about then. He didn't look well. "Y-you knew!"

"Well, not straight off, but . . ." I dragged in some air and got this false kind of a chuckle happening. "Dad, wait till you hear the story. You're gonna love this." I went on to tell him the story, highlighting the hilarious bits. I ended with, "And isn't that just the biggest riot you've ever heard in your entire life? Ha! Ha!"

Call it instinct, but I knew the guy wasn't with me on this one. The clue might have been that he hadn't cracked one tiny grin and that his face was turning purpler by the second.

"Dad, I don't know how to tell you this, but that mustard-colored sweater does nothing for the color of your face at the moment. Perhaps you should save it for times when your blood pressure is more even. . . ."

"Josephine, how can you not take this seriously?"

"Inherited stupidity?" I offered.

"That's it! You obviously aren't fit to be let out! This boy has lied, cheated, enticed you into bars, and who knows what else! I can't believe how irresponsible you've been. Your mother obviously lets you run wild!"

I'd opened my mouth to defend Frew, but suddenly I was taking this very seriously. Dad had gone too far. That crack about Mom was the lowest. He could do what he liked and say what he liked about me or even Frew—but he'd better leave her alone! "Don't you dare criticize Mom—at least she's there for me!"

"And just what do you mean by that? What do you call this vacation? Do you know how much this has cost me in time and money? And all for you!"

"Crap!" I yelled back.

"Watch that mouth, young lady! That's it, Josephine. I forbid you to see that instructor again, and you are not to leave the Chalet until you've learned a lesson."

He stomped off, but through my tears I had the last say. "You think I care? You haven't hurt me, Dad! You can't hurt me anymore. You have to love someone before they can hurt you. . . ."

Chapter Seven

Food and any other sustenance forgotten, I raced to my room and grabbed my gear. There was no way that I was going to let this guy tell me how to run my life! Especially when this was the same guy who couldn't have cared less whether I was dead or alive for most of the past three years. What's worse, I blamed myself. Don't they say that if you wish for something hard enough then you get it? For years I wanted my dad to remember that he had a daughter. Well, he'd finally remembered. But he knew her only by sight. My father had no idea *who* Josephine Mary Vincent really was. . . .

My first instinct was to ring Mom, but I figured that was a copout. One of the things that Mom and I had going for us was that she trusted me to work things out. She encouraged me to stand on my own two feet. She wouldn't have minded if I rang, but for some weird reason I knew it was important for me to see this thing through alone—even if the result was that I decided that my father could hop into his fancy car and drive off into the sunset forever.

I tried to fight them, but fresh tears started pouring down at this thought. I told myself again that I didn't care; that I didn't really love him; that I was just crying because I'd faced the end of a dream. Yeah, that was it. I mean, I'm the kid who still put cake out for Santa Claus, aren't I? I've just never have been able to let go of a dream.

I guess it was easier to try to convince myself that I didn't love the man than to accept that he didn't love me.

I thought about his ultimatum and nearly laughed out loud. At least I would have if there'd been a laugh in me. Telling me I couldn't leave the Chalet was a joke. Who did he think was going to be there to police it? God knew what my father and Kate got up to all day, but they were never around the Chalet—unless it was to tell me what to do!—till dinnertime. And they'd never invited me to join them. Not once. Okay—so I may not have accepted the offer, but it would have been really nice to get asked!

At the front door I wrapped my scarf right up around my face and pulled my goggles into place—even though I didn't even have skis on.

Storming down the steps I thought about the fact that I'd never openly defied either of my parents, but I figured this was different. Until my father recognized the whole me as his daughter, then I didn't have to recognize his rules. And if deep inside me I didn't quite believe all that stuff, well, I figured it was just a matter of time.

I found Frew at the main chairlift just as he was about to take off to the top with a group of medium-level skiers.

"Hi!" It was easy to put on a cheerful act; between ski goggles, scarves, and hats, it would have been pretty impossible for him to pick up on the fact that I'd been bawling my eyes out for the past hour! And anyway, red noses were a fact of life around here. "Am I allowed to join your group?"

"Sure! Actually it'll be really good for you. We're skiing the seven mile run back to Pine Flat and—"

"Seven miles!" I needed to burn some energy and get lost for a while. But did I need to do seven miles' worth?

"Don't panic; it's a beginner's trail. Nice, easy slopes—but it gives you the space to really get going. A lot of it is downhill. You'll love it."

He'd been right about one thing: it would be really good for me. Fresh air and exercise would have to help in some way. Isn't that what oldies are always saying? That the great outdoors is the cure for everything? But more important than that, it would keep me out of everybody's way—for quite a while! And I needed that more than anything.

I hung back with Frew, where he was keeping an eye on the rest of the group. He was right; it was a fairly easy run, and the scenery was pretty spectacular. Everyone was having a ball, and if I hadn't been so uptight about everything else it probably would have been fun. Still, it took a while to recover my breath, so we were actually back on the courtesy bus before I got the chance to talk to him.

"You did good today!" He smiled with the compliment, and I wished that I were in a better mood to receive it.

"Yeah, thanks. It was cool."

He frowned. "You've been quiet today. Any probs? Those idiot mates of mine didn't put you off last night, did they? They're really harmless, you know. A bit free-spirited—but they're decent blokes."

I shook my head. Even his accent and Aussie-isms weren't working their magic today. "Nah. They're cool. In fact, they're really great!"

He turned and looked straight into my face. "Is that it? You prefer one of them to me?"

I shook my head.

"Both of them?" he spluttered.

"Neither of them. I like you. You're my choice. But . . ."

"But?"

I swallowed deeply. "Look, this is hard. But will you be devastated if we have to cancel the dinner with my father and his latest girlfriend tonight?"

His eyes narrowed. "Nah. How come?"

This was it. Better let him have it—at least part of it. I'd already decided to keep Dad's opinion of Frew to myself. "Dad went right off today about me being at the bar last night."

"Hell! Jeez, Jo! It's all my fault! I'll go and see him as soon as we get back."

"No, don't!" I tried to swallow the panic pumping through me. "I mean, that's really cool of you and everything; it's just that there are a few other problems as well. Believe me, it'll probably just make things worse."

"What happened? Tell me, Jo. If I've caused any problems for you then I'll make them right. I'll explain. Look, I picked up that you and your dad aren't that close, but surely this is something you can work out. He *is* your dad."

"Not that you'd notice." I sighed, hating that I sounded so sorry for myself. "Forget I said that. It's pretty complicated." It was hard talking about it, and harder trying to explain it to anyone else, especially when I didn't understand it properly myself. I turned back from the scenery blurring past the window. "It's just that it seems like I've been waiting forever for my dad to notice me, and now that he has, it's like a dream turned into a nightmare. It'd serve him right if I did something really stupid. . . ."

Frew shook his head. "That sounds like a pretty dumb move to me. Decisions like that usually only hurt the person who made them."

He waited, probably for me to come to my senses and agree. I didn't, not in the mood I was in, so he went on talking. "How did your old man find out where we were?"

I gave a half laugh. "That dropkick Justin told him. He's staying at the Chalet. He's been giving me a hard time since I got here."

This time Frew groaned really loudly. He swore, too, not really loudly . . . but really bad. "I told those guys to go easy on him! Oh, jeez, Jo! I've really sunk you in it."

"What on earth are you talking about?"

"After we took you home last night, we passed the bar and there was the cretin, Justin, hassling this other chick. He was all over her, and it was pretty obvious she was a bit scared. So Graham and Rob kind of pushed him around a bit. They didn't exactly hit him or anything, but they warned him off. He wasn't happy. Didn't like being told what to do—and especially for the second time that night. I'm guessing that maybe telling on you was his way of getting back at us. . . ."

I nodded. "Yep, that sounds like wimpy Justin.

But I don't think he needed a reason to get back at me. He's been trying to get at me all week. And don't be sorry. The guy deserved all he got and probably more. Actually, I'm really glad that you guys saved that girl. If only my dad could see past someone's bank balance, he might actually see there are some decent people in the world who don't have six-figure monthly incomes!"

"Pardon? I don't get it."

"Forget it. My dad has some pretty weird ideas. And don't worry about making things worse for him and me. I've got a feeling that it was all going to hit the fan soon anyway. This vacation was just a perfect setup for it. All it took was for us to be together in one place for more than a couple of hours."

Frew leaned over and put his arm around me. "Hey, I'm really sorry, mate. But cheer up; things can only get better."

The guy was a sweetheart. I knew he was trying to make me feel better—he just didn't realize that it was an impossible task.

"How about your video?"

I swiped at my eyes and forced a smile. "My video? I haven't been to pick it up yet. They had to dub it with some background music. I've kinda lost interest."

He just nodded and squeezed my hand. Other guys I've known would have tried to take advantage of a situation like this—you know, where the girl is feeling pretty lost and vulnerable. They'd move in. But not Frew. Frew just pressed my head into his shoulder and let me lie there till we reached the village. It felt so good. He probably would have died if I'd told him, but even as romantic as it all was, it really made me miss my mom.

Was I a loser or what?

When we finally climbed off the coach I gave him a little peck on the cheek. He didn't push for anything more, just gave me a big hug.

He started to argue, but I didn't let him walk me back to the Chalet. That was the other thing about Frew: he didn't try to press his own will on you. If you really felt strongly, he went along—even if he thought he knew best. I really liked that. My dad could take lessons. . . .

My decision to go home alone wasn't made because I was caving in to my dad or anything, but it just made more sense not to rub Frew in his face. There was just about nothing more Dad could do to hurt me, but I certainly didn't want him messing with Frew's life.

Back inside I bypassed everybody and all the main rooms and just hid out in my own room. Dad wasn't there waiting with the whips and chains, so obviously he had no idea I'd deliberately disobeyed him all day. Obviously he also hadn't thought to ask the staff if I was okay. Go, Dad.

I couldn't be bothered with dinner. All my energy had been drained. Even my cell phone lay unused. Somehow none of it mattered anymore.

The knock on my door a couple of hours later startled me.

"Come in." I was lying on one of the beds trying to get interested in a dumb article on hair-replacement therapy. The whole scene was a fairly accurate statement about the level of my boredom and interest in the world. I looked up expecting to see Kate or even Dad, but instead Franz, the manager, poked his head in the door.

"Jo, there's a young guy downstairs waiting for you."

"Yeah?" I'd figured without asking that it must have been Frew and wasn't even embarrassed by the pathetic tone in my voice as I made for the door. I was already halfway across the room when the brain finally kicked into gear. "Oh . . . um . . . by the way, Franz, is my dad around?" I tried to act as casual as possible.

The last thing I needed was Franz to cotton on to the fact that I wasn't supposed to be seeing Frew and go all paternal on me.

Franz frowned. "They've gone out with the Woodses. Didn't you know that?"

That one hurt. "Oh, sure," I lied. Wound number 569 had just found its mark. It was a scar that wasn't going to heal anytime soon. Okay, my dad was mad at me, but he was my only real contact here at the darned place! He was my parent! He was my person! And he hadn't even bothered to come and see if I was okay. I didn't think I'd ever felt so alone. . . .

Franz was still watching me. The lump in my throat eventually started to shift with lots of prompting, and I finally found my voice. "I was just going to ask him something before he left, but I must have missed him."

Franz was pretty cool and I liked him a lot, but I don't think I fooled him. He put out a kindly hand, but I just shrugged and smiled at him. "No sweat. Truly! It was nothing—I can ask him tomorrow."

Franz just nodded and let me go past. I hoped he put my erratic behavior down to the general assessment that teenagers are by definition supposed to be weird.

Anyway, I left him to work out that problem and raced down the stairs, nearly taking out poor Frew and a coatstand as I threw myself at him. It was just too good to see him! If ever I needed a friend it was at that very moment.

"That's the problem with you, Jo," he joked dryly. "You're too uptight. . . . You should let yourself go. Express yourself more freely!"

I watched without pity as he untangled himself from the coats and lethal-looking hooks that had somehow missed skewering him. "Don't whine!

Millions of guys all over the world would be spun out to receive a greeting like that from their woman. . . ."

Frew stopped fighting with a particularly stubborn coat and stared at me for a second. A grin slowly spread across his face. Love that grin. "*Their* woman, eh . . . ?"

I grinned back, suddenly shy. "How come you're here, anyway?" I asked, hoping he didn't wonder too much about the fact that my face must have been bright red.

He answered by dragging something out of the deep pockets of his heavy outdoor coat and presenting it to me with a low bow.

"My video!"

His smile widened; he was obviously pleased with my reaction. "I thought we might watch it together. Would your dad mind? Maybe I could ask him?"

The mention of Dad twisted the knife in the wound a little more sharply. "He's not here, so we can't ask him. But take it from me—I don't think he'd care one way or the other what I do."

"Jo?"

I smiled. "It's okay—I don't want to talk about it. The important thing is that you came—and I'm crazy about that. Let's watch this video!"

He grinned back, even if it was a bit uncertainly.

Then he shrugged. "Okay, then—is there a machine here?"

I tracked down Franz's wife, Gail. "The television room is all yours," she confirmed. "Would you believe that everybody has gone out tonight, so you can watch to your heart's content. No one is going to be bugging you for a turn. I'll get Franz to light the fire in there."

By the time we were ready to settle down, everything was so cozy. The fire was crackling, the door was closed against chilly drafts, and the room was as warm as toast as we snuggled up beside each other on the big, soft, old fashioned sofa.

"Let's turn the overhead light off, Frew; I love firelight and I don't see it much. The West Coast climate doesn't really call for open fires a lot."

The video was a hoot. The background music was from the movie *Pretty Woman*, which made the whole thing really wild. There were a couple of great shots of Frew showing me what to do and then they'd pan to me seemingly doing the opposite! Talk about uncoordinated—I'd made it an artform! And this had been my best day!

Occasionally I looked really smooth, and I accepted Frew's compliments that one day I might make a really great skier until he added, "Not that I expect to live long enough to see it!"

The rat!

"This is war!"

He'd had the sense to try to hide behind a pillow, which protected him from the one I was pounding him with. I lunged at him, tearing at his shield. He answered with a waist tackle that sent us crashing onto the floor. He was absolutely cracking up as we wrestled on the floor of the darkened room. Even though we were only messing around I think I surprised him with my strength. He might have been winning, but it wasn't all his way. I made him work for it.

In a move that would have made a professional smile, Frew managed to get me under him. With a typically male caveman-type roar he claimed victory—much to my disgust!

We were both puffing and giggling when it happened. Suddenly everything changed . . . it sort of sneaked up on us. Like, there we were just kidding around, having innocent fun, when what we were doing dawned on us both at the same moment. Man, it was so dramatic. We just stared at each other. . . .

I can't blame Frew; I knew he was going to kiss me, and I kind of met him halfway. This was serious, I could tell by the way he kissed me. He was shaking.

Thoughts of my parents flew into my head—my father . . . my father's face. The same old fear—my father wouldn't love me. Just as quickly my mind answered, *But he doesn't really love you anyway.*

He doesn't even know the real Josephine. . . .
What would he care? He thinks you're wild, unta-
med. He probably wouldn't even be shocked . . .
or would he?

That last thought unleashed a little devil in me.
Somehow I'd crossed an invisible barrier. I'd made
a decision. For all the stupidest, dumbest reasons
that I wasn't game to look too carefully at, I'd made
the decision.

Frew and I stared at each other again. This was
a big one for him, too. He looked a bit scared. I
knew how he felt. I didn't know how to do this. I
nodded, barely moving my head. My mind half registered the background music—the video . . . Na-
talie Cole . . . "Wild women do, and they don't
regret it. . . ."

It was a sign.

His hand moved to my waist.

"How's the video going? Oh! I guess I should
have knocked!"

"Gail!"

"We . . . er, that is Franz and I just made some
hot chocolate and popped some popcorn. I, er
don't suppose you want any . . . ?"

We'd leaped from the floor as if it had suddenly
caught fire. I knew my face had! I stared at the
loaded tray, trying to bring my mind back into focus. Frew had dived into a chair, a pillow placed on
his lap, and watched silently as Gail plonked the

tray on a coffee table. Heck! I had to say something! "I . . . er . . . We were, er . . ."

Gail's face turned to me and I caught her expression in the firelight. She was trying not to laugh! Her voice was kind. "It's okay, honey; we've all stolen kisses in the dark."

After she left Frew let out a huge sigh. "Do you think she'll tell your father what we were doing?"

"Actually we weren't doing anything much."

"Yet," Frew answered grimly. "Jeez, Jo, do you realize how close we came? Man, when I think of how your old man must have it in for me already . . ."

In an instant the anger was there again, full-blown and ready to burn. "Give me a break, will you? What I do hasn't got anything to do with my father. This is *my* body, and I'll make the decisions about it. And I don't give a damn what he thinks! As matter of fact, it might shock him into taking some real notice of me; then he could either accept me as I am or walk away. Either way I'd know."

There was silence in the room for what seemed to be forever. Awful silence. Deadly silence.

Finally Frew asked, "Is that what all this was about tonight, Jo? Getting back at your old man?"

I didn't answer. I just sat and stared into the fire. He moved; I could feel him coming closer to me. I wanted to tell him that I was a bitch. That I was sorry. That I'd gotten confused. That I really liked him but . . . Somehow no words came out. Because he knew the truth. And I'd never hated myself more in my entire life.

He stood in front of me; I had to look up.

"Frew? I . . ." I put my hand up to take his but he stepped away.

I don't know what he thought I was going to say, but it didn't take an Einstein to guess.

"No way, Jo," he answered in a voice that I barely recognized. "What was it you said a minute ago about your body? Well, man, that cuts both ways. . . . This is *my* body and I'll make the choices about it. No one likes being used. It was nice knowing you. See you around."

Chapter Eight

My face burned. Until this moment I hadn't known what embarrassment really was. Oh I'd made a fool of myself plenty of times—but never to this level. This was an all-time high. Another personal best.

What happened here, anyway? How did the tables get turned on me? Okay, so I'd been an idiot—but what happened to male hormones raging out of control? I tried to get angry. Weren't guys supposed to think with their lower anatomy? That's what my best friend's mom told us. It's supposed to be us girls who do the dumping! It's supposed to be us girls who are the ones in control!

But going for angry and indignant didn't work. I'd gone past embarrassment; I was humiliated—too humiliated even to be angry. I could still see the hurt look on his face, especially when he thought that I'd wanted us to start all over again . . . to take up where we'd left off. I felt the heat really soaring through my body. He'd never believe that I'd changed my mind.

If I hadn't felt so rotten it would have been laughable. I couldn't think of one other guy who would have been ticked off because he thought I'd wanted him to make love to me! Mind you, that said a lot about the circle of friends I hung out with.

Frew certainly seemed to be a better class of person. Maybe they did things differently Down Under. His last words echoed in my mind. Oh, Lord, I hated that he knew I was going to use him to get back at my father.

But, my conscience answered, *isn't that what you were doing?*

Yes! No! I silently argued. I really liked Frew, more than I've liked any other guy. I jumped up in a burst of nervous energy and started to pace the room.

Then why didn't you run after him? Why didn't you explain?

I threw my arms up over my head, I wanted to stop the voices. Or maybe I just wanted to avoid the answers. "Because . . . because," I yelled at the empty room, "because I couldn't! Because I *was* going to use him! Not deliberately, not in cold blood, like he thought. But," I ended in a whisper, "what makes it really lousy is that I really do like him . . . so much."

First Dad and now Frew! Obviously I'm just destruction on legs when it comes to relationships.

I threw myself onto the lounge and curled up in a ball. I didn't think I'd ever felt so sorry for myself; I know I'd never howled my eyes out quite like that before.

That was where Dad and Kate found me. Kate rushed straight over and wrapped her arms around me. She didn't ask any questions or say anything. We just hugged. Dad just stood there, shifting from one foot to the other, looking at me as though I'd grown an extra head. It was Kate who got me into bed; my dad still hadn't said a word.

My first thought the next morning was that I was in some kind of weird time warp. All the yelling and screaming sounded just like my folks before the divorce! Funny—it was a sobering thought. I'd hated those days. . . .

As soon as I remembered where I was I got up and wandered into the hall. I hadn't even bothered to get dressed; my one concession to modesty had been to throw a big football sweatshirt over my flannel PJs.

It was absolute chaos out there. It seemed like everybody in the whole place was crammed into that hallway. Most of them were in their nightclothes, except my dad. He must have pulled on the clothes he'd worn the night before, because he looked a bit rumpled. Certainly not the smooth look my father usually liked to project.

Gail and Franz were both there, looking really nervous. Mrs. Woods was there in her jammies too, these long white satin things . . . pretty classy. I avoided thinking about the striped men's version under my sweater.

It was Mrs. Woods doing all the screaming. Justin was playing the model son by having his arm around her, trying to comfort her. Mr. Woods was the one doing all the yelling . . . most of it for the police.

I moved closer to Kate. "What's up?"

"Cynthia Woods has lost her diamond bracelet. She thinks someone has stolen it."

"Yeah?" I suppose I should have sounded more interested, but I'd already figured that it'd been a dumb move to wear it around here anyway.

"Frank Woods is demanding that everybody's room be searched," Kate went on, "and obviously Gail and Franz aren't too happy about that."

"No, I 'spose not," I answered on a yawn. "I guess they can see irate customers leaving here in droves. Funny how rich people think they can tramp over everyone else." I yawned again. "*And* wreck their sleep. I'm going back to bed. Don't wake me if they find it. I can live without that knowledge till I'm conscious again." Actually I could live without that knowledge forever. Compared to my life the whole thing was pretty trivial.

After the heavy scene last night and all the bawling, I was wiped out. I'd slept fairly well, all things considered. I remembered only one dream: I must have been little again, and I was crying about something, and Dad was there hugging me and telling me that everything was okay. I guess that's why dreams are called dreams—they're just the opposite of reality.

But being wiped out wasn't the only reason I wanted to go back to bed. Call me a coward, but I wasn't looking forward to seeing Frew. I guessed I'd have to face him sometime, but this morning wasn't that time. The thought crossed my mind that we had only a couple of days left, and I could probably avoid him until then. But even though last night still made me feel sick when I thought about it, I couldn't just leave and not see him just once more. I had to least try to explain that I wasn't that kind of girl.

I wasn't quite sure why his opinion of me mattered that much—we'd probably never see each other again after this—but still, it did. Frew was a nice guy. A good guy. I wanted him to know that I was okay, too. It was important. It was also going to be one of the hardest things I'd ever do. I definitely needed to sleep on it some more.

When I finally did wake up again it was close to noon and I had the worst headache I'd ever had. I rolled over, wondering whether I might just as well stay there for the rest of the day, when a slight movement at the side of the room caught my attention. "Dad? What are you doing here?"

He was sitting in one of the big armchairs, leaning forward, his arms resting on his legs. He looked tired. At my question he looked up, but his eyes were cold. I pulled the covers tighter around me, wondering what was coming. His voice matched his eyes. "What in the hell was that boy doing here last night?"

Help! Gail *had* told him what we'd been doing or at least what we'd been about to do. "Um . . . he brought my video up for us to watch."

I didn't have a clue what to say next. Kate saved me. She popped her head in at that moment, and with her help I managed to convince him that I'd be able to think more clearly after a shower and some coffee.

Those things completed, I wished that my prediction had been right. But unfortunately nothing had changed. My head was still pounding and I could barely think at all. We were back in my room and Dad was still demanding the answers to the same questions.

"Gee, Dad, it was all really innocent."

"Josephine, you were strictly forbidden to see that boy!"

"But Dad, he's really cool; I really like him. We didn't do anything wrong!"

"Where did you entertain him?"

"We were in the television room. See? How much could we have gotten up to in the television room?" I laughed weakly. Lordy—if only he knew how much you *could* get up to in the television room!

"Did you come up to your room at any time?"

"No!" I answered in a voice that told him I'd never do anything like that. I'm glad he couldn't see the fingers crossed behind my back!

"How far *did* you go?"

"Far?" I asked in a squeaky voice. "Far?"

"Yes, *far*, Josephine! Come on; you're not stupid."

"Not far at all," I answered, finding it harder to breathe by the second. "We were only on the floor because—"

"Which floor?"

"The television room floor."

"Was that the only floor you were on?"

I was starting to get worried. Was my dad kinky? Did he have a secret floor fetish that I didn't know about? I was dumbfounded for a second. I just stared at him.

"Oh, for goodness' sake, Josephine! It is obvious to me that only one unauthorized person was in this building last night, but if you'd rather talk to the police and tell *them* which floors you were on . . ."

The police? Were they kinky too?

Blame it on the headache, but it had taken this long for me to realize that my father and I had been having two different conversations. Relief that my dad and the police weren't interested in my sex life—nonexistent as it was—was momentary. It was replaced by cold shock.

"Wh-what do you mean?"

"I need to know your exact movements last night. We're going to have to know exactly how far into the building that boy was able to get. And if you saw him on this floor or just downstairs on the first floor."

"What are you talking about? You can't believe that Frew stole that bracelet!" I stopped and really looked at the set look on Dad's face. "Jeez! You really *can* believe it, can't you! You've got your mind made up!"

"I'm just facing facts, Josephine. Gail told us that everybody was out except you and this Frewin fellow. You've already told me that he comes from a poor family."

"And we all know how untrustworthy the poor are!" I finished sarcastically.

"Josephine, you're putting words into my mouth. I've never said that. I'm not even what you'd call excessively wealthy myself! But there are

other facts. He lied to you about his name; he—"
No doubt Dad would have gone on, but the door
burst open at that moment and Mr. and Mrs.
Woods barged in.

"At least poor people probably knock. . . ." I
mumbled, causing another filthy look to pass from
my father to me.

"Well, you're finally awake, young lady! Perhaps
you will tell us the exact name of this thief that
you've been hanging around with." That was Mr.
Woods—nobody could ever accuse him of good
manners.

"Frewin is not a thief!"

"Frewin! Yes, that's it!" Mrs. Woods turned her
fake blond head to her husband. "When I met
them in the village, he fairly drooled over the bracelet."

"But that doesn't make him a thief!"

"But he *is* the one with the opportunity." Mr.
Woods was acting like some stupid television lawyer. He turned on me really quickly, almost scaring
the life out of me. "Can you tell us that he wasn't
out of your sight for even a second?"

I hesitated, not because I thought that Frew was
guilty, but because I wasn't with him for the entire
time. I mean, he'd been in the foyer waiting on his
own, but then Franz would have seen him if he'd
come up the stairs. But what about when he left?
I hadn't gone out with him, and I'd been so spaced

out that I hadn't heard the door shut behind him.

"See!" Mr. Woods was doing a great imperson-ation of a bad actor pretending to be a lawyer. "See!" he yelled. "That proves it! She can't tell us that she was with him the entire time!"

This was turning into a kangaroo court—in more ways than one. I figured that if they got their hands on Frew at this moment they'd hang him from the nearest oak tree. An Aussie tried at his own kan-garoo court here in the democratic U.S. of A. Something was very wrong with that scene. "Dad?" I pleaded.

Dad hung his head.

"There's no use asking your father to intervene; he agrees with us. He told us that this young man desperately needs money for something or other. So therefore he not only had the opportunity, but a motive for the crime," Mr. Woods answered.

I kept staring at my father. "Dad, that was pri-vate information! And those things Frew said, a-about being German. It was a scam! You know, just a game! Come on, Dad, didn't you do stuff like that when you were young? Kid around? Scam to attract girls? Everyone does it! It doesn't mean he was bad. He's not a liar or a thief, Dad. Please listen to me! I know him!" But my father didn't react. I might as well have kept my mouth shut. I felt so betrayed. He'd never been there much for me, but this was over the top. He was letting these people walk all over me. My opinion didn't count.

Sadly, in my dad's eyes, it probably never had.

I turned to the Woodses and said the only other thing I could think of: "I thought in this country you were innocent until you were *proven* guilty. Where's your proof?"

Frank-baby shuffled and puffed himself up a bit taller. "Well, we, er . . . don't have it yet. But you've helped us greatly. I'm sure it will be just a matter of time. The police will be very interested in the information you've provided."

My heart gave a huge jerk. "But if the police start questioning Frew about this, he might lose his job! And if he loses this job then he'll lose his chance to get to go to the Olympics!"

"He should have thought about that before he stole the bracelet."

"He didn't steal the bracelet! Read my lips!" I felt like stamping my feet. "I can't believe you people! What sort of people are you, anyway? You have no proof, yet you are quite prepared to destroy someone's life! And what if by some miracle you find out that someone else stole it, or that Mrs. Woods left it in some bathroom when she was washing her hands? What then? How do you make it up to Frew then? Just get out of this room . . . all of you!"

"Josephine!"

"Stuff it, dad! You go too! This is my private

space, and you all make me sick! Frew is worth ten of you lot!"

Dad opened his mouth to have another go at me, but a tap on the door saved me.

"Come in," I barked, losing some my aggravation when I saw who opened the door. "Hi, Franz, come and join the party. By the way, you've got really nice manners. My mother taught me that it's very polite to knock. I just thought I'd tell you that." If the Woodses took offense to that, then as far as I was concerned that was great!

"Hi, Jo." His face looked pretty grim as he nodded to everybody else. "Um, Jo, there's someone downstairs for you." He looked really sorry that he'd had to say that in front of the crowd, or at least that's what I took it to mean.

Frew! I had to get to him before this lynch mob got their hands on him. In one really neat move I bounced from my bed to the next and onto the floor, and was out the door before most of them realized what was going on.

At the bottom of the stairs I whispered as loudly as I was game, "Get out of here quickly!"

Frew might have been intuitive last night, but today he was pretty dense. "Jeez, Jo, I know I acted like a jerk last night and that you must be pretty ticked off with me, but I thought you'd cut me a little bit of slack!"

Through all this I was madly looking over my

shoulder, waiting for the troops to come barging down the stairs. "Look, just listen to me! Get out of here, will you? Scram!"

"Give me a break, will you? I've had a lump in my gut the size of Tasmania about coming here. I—"

Ooooh! I could hear them coming! Frowning at him, this time I really did stamp my feet. "Too late! Man! Why didn't you listen to me?"

"Josephine! We want to talk to that young man, and so will the police!" It was almost comical watching Mr. Woods, all red-faced and puffy as he led the brigade down the stairs.

"The police?" Frew's face showed no fear, only puzzlement. I was hoping like hell that they all noticed that fact.

I jumped in to explain: "Frew, Mrs. Woods's bracelet is missing."

"So?"

"So they think . . . you might have seen something last night." Standing there looking at him, remembering all the good things he'd done this week, the fun we'd had, the friend he'd been to me, I swallowed. There was no way I could tell him that they thought he was a thief.

Behind me, Mr. Woods snorted. "It's all right Josephine; we'll take over from here. Justin, ring that detective and tell him we have the suspect here, if he'd like to come and question him."

I saw Frew jump. "Suspect! What in the hell is going on here?"

He looked at me in amazement. "Boy! When someone pisses you off they really cop it, don't they! And to think I came here to apolgize! Thanks a lot!"

This was no time to take offense; the Woodses were ready to lock him up and throw away the key. "Listen to me, you idiot! I've just spent the last hour proclaiming your innocence, so stuff the accusations or I'll just turn you over to Batman, Robin, and Catwoman here!" I answered, indicating old Frank and Justin, who were hanging over Frew like vultures over a corpse, and Mrs. Woods, who was patting her face—obviously worried that the face-lift marks were showing. They made me sick! All of them.

A stupid grin spread across his face. "Really? You did that for me?"

That grin. "Yeah," I answered, feeling suddenly so much better. The very fact that he was here meant that there was a chance that we could put all that garbage from last night behind us. This was Frew, my friend, standing here in front of me. I grinned back. "An insensitive baboon you may be, but I know you're not a thief."

"Ahem . . ."

Frew and I both turned to face Mr. Woods. Actually I'd almost forgotten that the others were even there, and I had a fairly good idea that Frew had as well. "I'm sure that we're all delighted that you're so keen to give this young man such a glowing reference, my dear; it's just a shame that you hadn't saved your enthusiasm for someone worthier."

"Worthier! Just who do you think you are? You're nothing but a jumped-up—"

"Josephine!" That was my father.

I turned on him too. "Don't you start! You're just as b—"

"Mr. Woods?" Gail interrupted. "The police are here. . . ."

Chapter Nine

I suppose the police just have a job to do. And I suppose they have to ask all those questions, and I don't suppose they deserved the garbage I gave them, but I'd had enough. I just hoped I hadn't blown it for Frew. It was looking more and more like I was his only hope. What had I landed him in?

They were talking to Frew now. Dad had asked me—no, make that *ordered* me—to get some breakfast from the kitchen (as if I could eat!) and then to stay in my room until they were finished. Poor Frew! I wondered what they were putting him through. Dad had no right to make me stay up here. I could feel the anger building stronger and stronger. It was like I might explode. Then again, maybe it was right that I should be stuck in my room. Because if I were face-to-face with any of those morons downstairs right now I'd—

The knock at the door was becoming a comical farce—but at least it put a stop to my bloodthirsty plans for mass murder. "What do you want?" I figured anyone who was game enough to knock on my door while I was in this mood obviously had a death wish, so they could take the heat.

"Open the door, Josephine!"

Dad! I swallowed the urge to tell him to get lost, but only because I was desperate to find out about Frew. "What have they done to him?" I asked, flinging open the door.

"The police have taken him back to his quarters so they can search for the bracelet."

"Jeez, Dad! What have you done? Frew will probably lose his job now! Why couldn't you just believe me? I told you that he didn't do it!"

"Stop yelling, Josephine. Everybody in the Chalet must be able to hear you."

"Why should I?"

"Because I'm asking you to." With that he came right into the room and closed the door.

"You're a joke, Dad! It must be really cool to be a parent and expect kids to do what they're asked, but never have to do what their kids ask. I just hope I never turn out to be a parent like you!" I was still yelling. I didn't give a damn about what anybody else thought.

When he answered his voice was quiet, but I could tell that he was really trying to hang on to his temper. "What have you ever asked me to do that I haven't done?"

I laughed, but it wasn't a very jolly sound. "Jeez, Dad, you must have plenty of time if you can hang while I recite the list!"

"I don't understand."

"All right—you want answers? I'll give you answers! For starters, I asked you not to leave Mom and me."

That one threw him. Actually it kind of threw me. For years I'd thought about saying those words, but I never really thought I'd have the guts.

"Josephine?" I could tell he was having trouble speaking.

Not me. I was still spewing in the worst way. "What? Can't handle the answers, Dad? Well, maybe you shouldn't have asked the question." Most of the anger was about Frew, but it was also about me and Dad and our whole family mess.

"Josephine, I'm sorry; we explained all that to you."

"No, you didn't, Dad. *You* never said a word. You left it all to Mom. You didn't ask *me* if I wanted a divorce. You didn't even tell me you were leaving me. You just left. I used to wish that you'd died; that way I'd know that you didn't leave me by choice."

"Oh, hell, Josephine. I didn't leave *you*. Your mother and I decided that we couldn't live together; it had nothing to do with you. I love you."

"Then why didn't you need me in your life any-more?"

"I did, I just . . . I guess I was busy trying to make a new life."

"Too busy for your daughter? But not too busy for all your other girlfriends? Do you even *know* how that made me feel? And what about last night? Do you know how alone I felt when you didn't even bother to speak to me or make sure I was okay after you'd unceremoniously grounded me? I had to find out from Franz where you even were! Do you know how alone and humiliated I felt? Do you? Do you ever think about me, Dad? Ever?"

"Oh, Josephine—"

"For God's sake! My name is *Jo*! Can't you even call me what everybody else calls me?"

"It's hard. *I* named you. I named you after my grandmother. She was a wonderful woman. I couldn't understand why you wouldn't want to share her name."

"It's got nothing to do with your grandmother and everything to do with *me*! Can't you see that? It's who I am. I'm Jo, your daughter—not Jose-phine, your grandmother!"

"I suppose I've been wrong about some things, but I've tried Joseph—Jo."

"Oh, sure, Dad. Like how hard? What about my

school musical last year? I had a *main part*, Dad and you didn't even bother to turn up! Even after I'd sent you an invitation and everything!"

"What can I say . . ." He dragged his hands through his hair, and he suddenly looked really tired. "I must have been really busy that night."

"*Four* nights. It ran over four nights." My voice sounded empty, kind of lifeless. I knew I'd run out of anger. That probably also meant that I was pretty close to tears.

Strangely enough I think Dad was too. "Oh, God . . . I sent flowers, at least. Didn't I?"

I didn't trust my voice. I simply shook my head.

"Oh," was all he could manage.

No one was speaking. The silence was awful. The lump in my throat was so huge that it was almost impossible to swallow, but I had to force it down. There were more things that had to be said.

"Ma-maybe it's my fault. I mean, if I'd been prettier or smarter or something then maybe you'd have wanted to visit me. I used to wonder what I'd done to make you not love me."

My dad swore—the worst I'd ever heard him swear—and he shook his head. "I can't believe I've been so stupid. Of course I love you! You must know that! You are my daughter, part of *me*. I've always thought that you *are* the prettiest and the smartest kid any father could have. But I guess I made a bad judgment call. I always thought that because you were all those things, because you were so, so . . . *together* that you didn't really need me."

"Every girl needs her dad, Dad. Maybe I expected too much of a father. I don't know; you always just seemed to either yell at me or ignore me. I kind of thought that a father could be your pal too; at least that's what I always wished for."

My dad didn't answer; he just hung his head.

I continued, "I always used to daydream that we'd do really dumb things together, you know, just mess around, and that we'd really crack up over stupid things. And even that we'd hug sometimes. I keep having this dream that I'm a little kid and I'm curled up on your lap and you're reading me a story. Every now and then y-you . . . k-kiss me on th-the head. . . ." Huge, fat tears were rolling down into my mouth. I could taste the salt, and I turned to get a tissue.

I felt Dad's hands on my shoulders as he turned me around to face him; he still didn't speak. Instead he hugged me into him so tightly that I thought I'd smother. I didn't care; I just really let go. All the tears that I'd kept bottled up inside me for years came bubbling out. "Oh, Daddy . . ." I sobbed.

Dad's own tears were drowning the front of my hair. "It's okay, baby; I'm here. I may be a bit late—but I'm here."

I felt myself being lifted up, and then we were

in an armchair, me on Dad's lap, just like in my dreams. I don't know how long I cried, but it was well and truly night by the time I raised my head and Dad and I started to talk again. I'm not sure what world Dad was in during those hours, but I'd like to bet that we were both in the past. Perhaps we each saw it a little differently than before.

"Feeling any better?"

I nodded.

"You know, Jo, those weren't dreams you've been having about us; they were memories. I've been sitting here reliving those times. Those times before things started to go wrong between your mother and me. And you are right . . . I've made us both miss out on a lot, especially a lot of hugging. I've been a fool, Jo, and I don't suppose I deserve another chance, but I'd sure like another go."

"What about you and Mom?"

"That's one thing I can't change, and I don't think your mother would want me to. Your mom and I only did one truly great thing, and that was to create you. Now our time as a couple is over, but thank God we still have you. And thank God you've had your mother; she's done a great job raising you. You are one terrific kid."

Maybe I was giving in too easily, but my dad had said some pretty powerful stuff, like that he loved me! And that he was sorry, and that he thought I was terrific and that he loved me . . . And that he loved me . . . A nice warm feeling started in my tummy and spread through my whole body.

"Yeah, well, I'm really glad that you think those things, Dad, but I have to admit that I haven't exactly been a contender for the kid-of-a-lifetime award. At least not lately. I've been feeding it to you, haven't I? I mean, jeez—I didn't even want to come on this trip. I fought Mom over it, and she had to blackmail me into coming. Can you believe that? How ungrateful is that? I'm sorry, Dad."

Dad drew in a deep breath and then let it out slowly. "If this is honesty time, perhaps it's time I came clean, too. Jo, I can't even take the credit for the idea for this trip. What makes it worse is that I've been throwing it up at you all week, trying to make out what a great father I am. I can see now what an idiot I've been."

I'd probably known it all along, but I just hadn't taken the time to register. Now it was pretty obvious. "It was Kate's idea, wasn't it? This whole trip was something she planned. But why? Why would she want your kid along?"

Dad sighed again. "She's a pretty terrific person, Jo. Kate's got this rather large, rowdy Italian family. They're crazy; they argue and fight all the time, but they love each other to pieces. Kate couldn't understand that I had a daughter that I hardly saw.

She's been trying to help me to understand teenagers, especially my own."

This time it was me who was silent and Dad who continued. "I've always known that I loved you, but Kate helped me to see that you could grow away from me if I didn't put in the effort. During this week I realized how right she was, so I started acting the way I thought a father should. But as usual I got it all wrong—and that just pushed us farther apart. Last night when we came home and you were so upset I don't think I've felt so low in my whole life. Even then, at first I didn't know what to do. Kate knew, but I didn't. It scared me, Jo. I should have known what to do—and I didn't have a clue."

I nodded. "That's funny, 'cause I had another dream last night, you know, about you being there to make me feel better. It seemed so real."

Dad looked a bit embarrassed. "I guess it's a bit late to start trying to convince you what a great guy I am, but that wasn't a dream last night, Jo. I was so worried about you that I spent the night right here in this armchair. You half woke through the night and you were whimpering, so I soothed you until you drifted back to sleep. You were right; it was just like when you were little. It was a good feeling."

"So that's why you were the only one dressed in the hallway this morning!"

Dad grinned. "Yeah!" The grin faded. "But then I blew it, didn't I?"

"You mean about Frew?"

Dad nodded.

I figured this might be my last chance, so I went for it. "Dad, Frew really is the greatest guy I've ever met. You've got to believe me when I tell you that there is no way the guy would be a thief."

"But how can you be so sure, Jo? You've known him less than a week."

"I can't explain it, Dad; it's a gut thing. But . . ." Man, this was hard. I had to go carefully. I put my hands up as a sort of warning. "Dad, now I don't want you to go getting really heavy on me over this, but last night . . . well, Frew and I . . ."

I felt Dad start to freeze me out. "Jo, you don't mean . . . ?"

Oh, God! What a conversation to have with your dad. I was definitely acting like a card-carrying loony. "No, Dad, we didn't. But I guess you should know that it was more thanks to Frew than to me. If we're still being honest here, I was kind of peeved with you."

"Oh."

"Oh" wasn't the answer I'd been expecting. I was wishing he'd help me out a bit more; after all, I was new at this father-daughter thing. Is this all that happens when you drop the next-to-biggest one on your father? Still holding my breath, I peeked a sideways look. Oh, no! The poor guy was shell-shocked! Maybe it was time to bail him out. "Um, Dad? Are you okay?"

"Yes," he squeaked. Then, "Ahem, I mean 'yes.'" Thankfully he found his normal voice. It helped me to remember then that all this father-daughter stuff was new to him as well, and I guess I'd dumped him with a pretty heavy beginning.

"Dad, I guess what I'm trying to say is that if a guy has those kind of morals, then I don't think that he's a thief."

"I suppose not." Dad had answered, but I didn't think he was really listening, not properly. His next question confirmed my thoughts. "Are you always this, er . . . frank with your mother?"

"Yes." I was puzzled.

"Now I think I understand why she keeps trying to tell me that parenting is harder than I thought." He was still looking pretty glazed.

Finally catching on, I answered, "Don't worry, Dad; I'll go easy on you at first. I promise you we'll leave the unprotected-sex discussion, the abortion-versus-adoption debate, and the what-constitutes-heavy-petting questions till at least next week."

Turning greener by the second, he answered weakly, "Gee, thanks, Jo . . ."

"Cheer up, Dad! Think of teenage-hood as one of your business deals. We'll negotiate each problem as we come to it. Anyway, I don't think I'll be too much of a bother. I've got too many other worries to be too much of a problem to you."

"Like what?" he asked.

"Like Frew. Dad, I'm really worried about what this will do to his future."

Dad stayed silent for a while, obviously thinking. "You really are convinced of his innocence, aren't you? He's obviously fairly important to you."

"Yes, he is, Dad, and it's really important that you trust my judgment on this."

Dad stared at me for ages. Finally he pulled me in close to him again. "How could a simple father argue with such blind loyalty? All right, you've won me, princess; from now on your Frew will have three of us on his side."

"Three of us?"

Dad sighed. "Yeah, Kate was on your side all along."

I answered Dad with a giant hug. He chuckled—and kissed me on the top of my head. My dad loved me.

Chapter Ten

"Hey, you two, is it safe to come in?" The whispered question was accompanied by a shaft of light as Kate opened the door.

Dad chuckled. "Only if you're wearing your water wings. Things got a bit soggy in here."

She crept forward anyway, angling her body so that she could see us in the light from the open doorway. Still cuddled up on Dad's knee, I looked up to see why she hadn't spoken, but she was just standing there with a stupid grin all over her face. She was aiming it at Dad, and when I looked up at his face it was covered by the same soppy smile.

"This is just wonderful," she finally whispered. "Oh, dear, I think I'm going to cry. . . ."

"Now there's an Italian for you, Jo; they're either laughing, yelling, or crying. How is a man supposed to cope?"

There was a really warm sound to his voice when he spoke of Kate, and I suppose I was just a little bit jealous. I tried to shove it aside. Kate wasn't a threat to my relationship with my father; she'd proven that. But now that I'd kind of found him again, it was going to be a little bit hard to learn to share.

It would have been easier if I'd known how Frew felt about me, but after the mess I'd landed him in he probably wasn't speaking to me. Thinking of him made me ask, "Have you had any news about Frew? Did the police give him a hard time?"

"All I know," Kate answered, "is that they've finished questioning him, and they didn't find anything at his quarters."

"So he is free! That has to be the proof they need for his innocence! Man! I told everyone that he didn't do it!" I jumped off Dad's knee in a sudden burst of energy and hit the light switch. "Oops! Sorry, Dad! Just keep your eyes covered—they'll adjust in a minute."

Kate plopped onto one of the beds. "I don't think it's quite that simple, Jo—about Frew, I mean."

"But it *is* that simple, Kate. Frew didn't do it."

Kate continued, "I'm sure it is to you, sweetie, but to the police he is still a suspect. They say it's possible that he might have hidden the bracelet or already gotten rid of it. Not finding it in his room didn't mean much."

"That has to be the most ridiculous thing I've ever heard! Why are they picking on Frew? It could have been any one of us! It could have been me! If Frew is a suspect then *I* want to be a suspect! Dad, tell Franz that I demand he search my room!"

I couldn't have missed the look that passed between Kate and Dad, and let out a megagroan. "I'm a bit late with my demands, aren't I? It's already been searched, hasn't it? Take a tip from me, will you—don't you pair ever sign up with the CIA; you'd never hack it! One look at your faces and the enemy would know the truth!"

"We're sorry, honey," Dad explained. "Everyone's room was searched when the police first arrived. I gave permission for your room while you were in the kitchen. I didn't mention it because I didn't want you any more upset than you already were."

It's amazing how the facts change the emotion. I mean, it had been fine for me to yell "equality" before I knew it had already happened. But now . . . "You mean someone has been through all my things? *All* my things? Even my Gs and push ups?"

Dad and Kate nodded together.

"Oh," was all I could manage. Suddenly being a suspect wasn't as noble as I thought it would be. Then just as suddenly I tried to shake myself out of this selfish feeling. "Man! I am a definite coward! Here I am worried about Franz seeing a few pairs of ratty underwear, and poor old Frew might have his whole future in shreds. Dad, I need to see him!"

"I don't think that's a good idea, Jo. When I spoke to the police, they said that Frew's boss was waiting to see him. They also said he was pretty upset. It's late and I've asked Gail to send some food up here for us, so I think it might be better to wait and see Frew in the morning."

Kate's voice was kind, and I knew that she was probably making sense, so I agreed, but it was a very reluctant agreement. As far as I was concerned, morning couldn't come quickly enough.

When it did, I hit the snowfields with a vengeance. No log nor building would be left unturned till I found Frew. No matter how he really felt about me, I had to let him know he wasn't alone. I had recent firsthand experience of what that felt like—and I really didn't want Frew to suffer.

An hour later, stomping the snow off my boots, I headed through the first floor of a big building, wishing my heartbeat would return to at least one-tenth its normal rate.

"Hi . . . I've been searching for you everywhere. I finally ran into Rob; he said to try here."

"Here" was the instructors' quarters, and I'd found Frew in a back room rubbing some stuff into his skis. I waited for a second, but he didn't answer.

"Hey, you're gonna rub holes in that ski if you don't let up."

He didn't move. "So what? I probably won't be using them much more anyway."

"Tell me something. Is it just me or is there an attitude in this room?"

Finally he turned to face me. "If an '*attitude*' is facing facts, then yeah, there's an attitude in this room."

"Sounds to me like you're giving up."

"Yeah! And what choice do I have? I've got that flamin' dropkick Woods family breathing down my neck! Not to mention your old man!" He'd spread his arms and they landed against his thighs with a dull thump. "You can see what happened here, can't you? The Woodses needed a fall guy. And I just happened to be in the wrong place at the right time."

Something clanged in my brain like an alarm, but I didn't take the time to examine it. I was too upset about Frew. "But they haven't proven anything! You're just a suspect like the rest of us! No one knows who did it!"

"Wake up and smell the coffee, Jo! The Woodses have decided that I'm their man! They're big shots with loads of money and they can make my life tough. They don't really care if I stole that blasted bracelet; they just want someone to blame!"

"But if they can't prove it, how can they hurt you?"

"Jo." Frew came over and put his hands on my shoulders. "Read my lips: They're hurting me already. My boss has pulled me off the roster until further notice."

"He what?" Is it possible for a heart to explode from overbeating? "He can't really believe that you *did* it!"

Frew sighed. "As a matter of fact, he says that he doesn't, but because I'm an employee he can't take any chances. Anyway, he reckons that it's better for me this way, 'cause if the Woodses start yapping to other customers then some of them might start complaining about me. And that's all I need. If I start getting any complaints coming in about me then I can kiss the Olympics and any chance of a sponsor good-bye forever. I can probably kiss it good-bye already."

I felt the heat rush through my body, my eyes started to burn, and yet another huge lump had landed in my throat. I was going for a record. I really didn't think it would be possible for me to feel worse than I did at that moment. *I'd* done this to him. I'd wrecked his dreams . . . his life. . . .

His body language said it all. It was like he'd given up. I bet he was wishing that he'd never met me; for his sake I wished he hadn't as well. But for my own sake I was glad he had. What a mess!

I didn't want to cry; apart from being a really lame female thing to do, I figured that I didn't have the right. As rotten as I felt, it wasn't my life that was getting destroyed; it was Frew's. I stretched my eyes open really wide and tried to think dry thoughts. It didn't work.

When the tears rolled down my cheeks, I half expected Frew to turn on me; after all, I was the destroyer, not the destroyee. If Frew's life was wrecked then it would be my fault. But whether he liked it or whether I liked it didn't matter; my mind and body thought that that was a heck of a good reason to cry. And there was nothing anybody could do to stop it.

I'm not sure whether it was the choking noises, gurgles, sniffles, or the need to change into dry socks that made Frew turn to me, but he did, and the look on his face just made me cry all the harder.

He crossed the room in a single bound—my very own crocodile hunter to the rescue.

"Hey, don't cry. It'll be okay," he whispered as he pulled me into a gianormous hug. "Don't cry for me. My dad reckons that I'm always going off my brain about things before I've thought them through."

The hug felt great, but it didn't help with my guilt, so I pushed away. "Don't, Frew. You're just saying that to make me feel better." Okay, even though I said the words I was still hoping in some wild way that he really meant that things would turn out okay. I looked up at him through blurry eyes, but even the blurriness couldn't hide the misery in Frew's eyes.

"This is really serious, isn't it?" I guess the whispered words weren't actually a question, because I knew the answer. Frew's nod confirmed the worst.

He threw his arm over my shoulder. "Come on, misery guts; let's go and make some coffee."

"Does this mean that we're friends again?"

"Do I have a choice?"

My answer was to dig him in the ribs. "Careful, my friend. Sympathy is a strange emotion; it can disappear very quickly. If you want me on your team you must learn to treat me with the proper respect!"

We'd made our way into the kitchenette, where he turned from getting the mugs out of a cupboard. I'd only been kidding around, but the look in his eyes told me that he'd remembered the night we'd been together at the Chalet. I could feel my face burning up, so I looked away.

"Jo?"

Just to add insult to injury those blasted tears started to well up again. Darn! Wasn't this one of the reasons I came here? To clear the air? To try to work things out? Didn't I always boast about being mature? And wasn't I always big on being up front about everything? Then why in the heck couldn't I turn around and talk to the guy about this?

A hand landed on my shoulder. "Jo, it's cool to be embarrassed. Man, I am! I nearly lost my guts, literally, twice before I turned up at the Chalet yesterday. I've acted like a total idiot!"

The fact that he blamed himself was enough to drag me out of my own misery. "Frew, you aren't! You didn't; I mean, you haven't! This is all my fault!"

I sat down at the little table. "You'd better make heaps of coffee—I've got a feeling that we're both going to need it."

He didn't sit down. He just leaned against the bench watching me. "How do you figure that?"

I wished he'd sit down; I felt like I was in school. "Well, you were right. . . ." I paused and licked my lips. "This is so hard! I guess I'm trying to say that the other night when we almost . . . you know . . ." Why couldn't I just come out and say it? I never figured that I had many hang-ups, but I was rapidly re-forming that opinion. Based on my present performance some psych doctor could make me her life's work!

"I haven't got a clue what you're trying to say, Jo, but let *me* say something. The other night I said some pretty lousy things, and I guess I didn't really mean them."

"You didn't?"

"I haven't figured it all out, but I think I blamed you because I'd acted like an idiot. It's pretty hard for a guy to admit that he hasn't had much experience with sex, but . . ." He stopped to take in a huge breath. "But apart from the odd grope in the back seats of the movies . . . I haven't. I've really got the hots for you, Jo, and I'm not saying that I didn't want to have sex with you. But on the floor, where anyone could have walked in on us? That's what I call really dumb! And here's the big one: neither of us thought about protection!"

"Oh, heck! My Personal Development teacher would expel me for sheer stupidity!"

"Yeah, to say nothing of our parents." He looked deadly serious for a minute; then he grinned. "You know, my old man has got this scheme for telling us guys about sex. He asks us to help him with the car or some farm machinery, and then when he's got you lying under tons of steel, like holding up a gearbox with your bare hands, and he's dead sure you can't nick off, he starts in our sex education!"

The visual thing was too much; I cracked up!

"Fair dinkum!" he went on. "I reckon that if I did something as dumb as not protecting the girl and myself after all those lectures, then my dad would accidentally on purpose let some huge motor fall right on top of me!" He cracked up with me then. "Not that he'd get much of a chance, though, I suppose. His plan has kinda backfired on him. These days, whenever Dad asks for any help with the machinery, us boys take off!"

I laughed with him; he was ripping on his dad, but I could tell it was in a nice way. "Your dad sounds cool."

"Yeah, I'm really lucky with my folks."

"Actually I've had a bit of luck with my own recently."

Frew answered by raising his eyebrows in question.

"Yeah, my dad and I have started to patch things up."

He started to smile, but I held my hands up to stop him from saying anything. There were other things I had to get cleared up. And it was now or never. I took a deep breath. "Frew, you have to know that the other night I think I *was* going to use you to get back at Dad. I don't mean that it was a conscious thing, and it wasn't till later that I admitted it to myself. As much as I think . . . that . . . well, it might have been great, I'm kinda glad we didn't. Over the years I've made lots of excuses for why I haven't 'done it,' but I think the plain truth is that I'm scared, and I figure that if I'm that scared then I'm not ready for it. Does that make any sense? And more important, do you hate me?"

"Girls aren't the only ones who get scared, Jo. I can relate to that. . . . It's okay." The words might not have been overwhelmingly convincing, but the smile that went with them made my day.

I smiled back. "Well, now that that's settled we have to work out what we're going to do about this jewelry-theft problem. Do you want my dad to go and talk to your boss?"

"Your dad! Go to bat for *me*?"

I wiped the coffee off my sweater, where it had unfortunately landed after Frew sprayed out his disbelief. "There's no need to say it like that! Yes, *my* dad! He's cool about you now and he wants to meet you properly. It's part of our new deal."

"Let me get this straight. You and your dad came to a deal about *me*, and you reckon he's changed his mind about me being a thief? Man, this *is* some new relationship you pair have! But if you don't mind, I'll reserve judgment until the jury brings back an innocent verdict."

"Suit yourself, but if you're not going to take his help then we have to try to solve this mess ourselves."

"*Our*selves?"

"Well, I kind of got you into this mess, so I guess it's only right that I try to help you out of it. What do you know about being a detective?"

"I've watched all the reruns of *Inspector Gadget*."

I punched him in the arm, trying to control my laughter. "This is serious!"

"I know it is, Jo," he answered in a very serious voice. "But don't you think it's time for a reality check? We don't know anything about trying to solve a mystery!"

"I know you've got more guts than that, Frewin Philpott. You must have determination if you're going to try out for the Olympics!"

He looked a tiny bit hopeful, and that made my own determination soar. "Well, I guess we could ask some questions, but I don't want to do anything that will make things worse."

"Okay! That works for me! So I figure the first thing we've got to do is to go and meet with my dad."

Frew gulped loudly. "Is this an absolute essential?"

I dragged him out of the chair. "Come on; you'll live. Jeez! What a transformation . . . from Superman to wimp in a few short hours!"

We took off before he could change his mind again. Back at the Chalet, Franz told us where to look, and it didn't take us long to spot them.

"Dad! Kate! Wait up!"

They'd been heading down toward the ski slopes when Frew and I caught up with them. They stopped, and I saw Dad's eyes narrow when he spied me with Frew. Kate must have noted the look as well, because I saw her whisper to Dad, who immediately plastered a forced smile across his face. Oh, well, it was a start.

(Note to self: Write to the pope or chairperson of the human resources department in charge of sainthoods and have him/her set aside one for Kate.)

"Dad, Kate, I'd like you to meet Frewin Philpott." I actually puffed rather than spoke the words. Jogging in the snow, I'd discovered too late, is not a recommendable pastime.

I made a big deal of slowing down my breathing. Despite the agreement between Dad and me, I was still pretty spaced out about this meeting. At first, focusing on my breathing was a cover—but as the seconds slipped by, I knew it was for real. It was that or hyperventilate!

It took Dad forever to finally put out his hand to shake Frew's. Just as well, because my lungs were about to collapse. "It's good to meet you at last, Frewin. Obviously Jo has told us a lot about you. She seems to think that we have done you a great disservice, and if we have, then I apologize."

Frew's reaction was so great that I almost grabbed him and kissed him right there—right in front of Dad! Man! I was sooo proud of him! He looked Dad straight in the eye and said, "It's good to meet you too, Mr. Vincent. Jo told me that she'd asked you to believe in me, and I think that was a pretty tough ask. I'd rather you make up your own mind about me, sir."

I watched with pride as Frew kind of pulled himself up a little bit taller and ended with, "I didn't steal anything, Mr. Vincent. I'm not a thief, and I never have been. Apart from my knowing that it's the wrong thing to do, my old man would disown me if ever I pulled a dumb stunt like that."

It was Dad's move. I watched him closely. He looked carefully at Frew's face. Frew just kept staring straight at him. After an eternity Dad seemed to come to a decision. He slapped Frew on the back. "Well, young man, either you're one hell of a con man or you're as honest as Jo seems to think. I can see why she's being so loyal to you, and for what it's worth you've won me as well."

It was one of *the* great moments in my life. I could feel my face glowing, and it wasn't caused by just the fact that it was almost frozen. A Snoopy dance was just begging to be set free! Good, gooey stuff just oozed out. "Guys . . . guys . . ." I babbled. "What can I say? This is just great!" My smile would be in place forever!

My dad cleared his throat. "Well, before you go getting too comfortable, Jo, I still have something to say. Okay, I don't believe that you're the dishonest type, but we still have to address what you pair almost got up to the other night."

"Dad!"

"Now, Jo, if I'm going to be a responsible parent then I'm going to have to take some responsib— Ahh! What was that? Ahh! Who did that?" Giggling from somewhere off to our right gave Dad his answer. He turned toward it just in time to collect another snowball in the side of the head.

"Dad, you're not going to be any fun if you just stand there and provide a stationary target. Throw a snowball back at her!"

Poor Dad, he'd never played much in his life; it had been all work. "But how?"

"Like this Mr. V." Frew had jumped straight in and molded a ball that he hurled straight back at Kate, catching her a beauty. He handed the next ball to Dad, who after a moment's hesitation threw it at Kate as well, cracking up when he caught her right on the backside.

Kate yelled in mock outrage as she tried to fend off snowballs from two directions. "Okay, if you guys want a war then let's make it a war of the sexes!" I yelled as I rushed over to Kate's side.

And war it was. I don't know what gave me the biggest thrill: the fun of playing with my dad like I'd dreamed of so often, or seeing Frew and Dad conferring head-to-head, working out their strategies. For one sad moment I wished that Mom could have been here, but I was beginning to understand some of the things between Mom and

Dad a little bit better. And besides, I had great memories of fun things that Mom and I had shared, and I knew she'd be thrilled to bits to know that I was finally chalking up one with Dad. . . .

Chapter Eleven

"Do you really think that snowman looked like Dad?"

"Before or after I dropped the snowball down his trousers?" Kate answered, throwing a look of pure devilment over her shoulder to where Dad and Frew were bringing up the rear.

"Before. I don't think anyone could re-create *that* look of horror!"

We'd reached the big main doors to the Chalet and were stomping off the loose snow. Dad and Frew had caught up, and Dad was really ragging on Kate about what he called her outrageous behavior. But even I could tell that he didn't mean it. They went inside and I went to follow, but Frew hung back.

"This place doesn't hold good memories for me, Jo. . . ."

"Yeah, I guess not. But things have changed; look how cool Dad is with you now. It'll be different; you'll see."

There's a saying about situations like this. I think it goes, "famous last words . . ."

I'd opened the door just in time to see Mr. Woods descend upon Dad like Homer Simpson on a pile of doughnuts. Frew was still hidden from view.

"Mal! Just the man I want to see. It goes without saying that I'm not happy about this thieving business. I don't like the way it's being handled at all. Now, I know that you and I agree that this young hooligan is guilty, and it looks like it will be up to us to prove it. What do you say? I think we should have a drink and talk it over."

I didn't doubt my dad for a minute. Well, maybe I did. But it was only for a second or two. Then Dad turned to me. "Jo, don't stand there with the door open; you're letting the heat out."

I panicked; I thought he meant that I had to shut the door on Frew, but his next words confirmed that my dad was for real: "And besides, Frewin must be freezing."

The look on Dad's face with ice in his pants was nothing compared to the look on Mr. Woods's face when Frew walked into the lobby.

"Mal? I hope you know what you're doing. This fellow is dangerous. Surely you have more concern for your daughter—to say nothing of your posses-sions—than to encourage him to hang around!"

I was a bit worried about my dad for a moment; he looked kind of old and tired. "Frank, I've made some stupid decisions in my life—worse than that, I've let other people make them for me; but I'm back on track now. You're right about one thing, though, and that is that there is a dangerous per-son in this lobby, but it's not young Frewin."

"I hope you don't mean what I think you mean, Mal. I thought you and I had a good business future . . . I'd be careful if I were you."

"Our business is off, Frank. We have no proof that the boy is guilty, and I won't help you destroy his future."

"You're going to be sorry that you uttered those words, Vincent! I'm going to call Franz now and have this lout thrown out of here!"

"Save your breath, Frank." The usually quiet Kate added her bit. "We're only here for a mo-ment; then we're all going out to dinner. What do you say to some thick steaks at the Boar's Head, kids?"

Dad grinned. "What a great idea! You'll forgive us for not inviting you, Frank. I don't think you'd enjoy our company. 'Bye!"

I almost split my sides trying not to laugh as Frank Woods huffed off up the stairs. As soon as he was out of sight I threw my arms around Dad. "You are the greatest! Did you see his face? Man, you can be on my team any day!"

Dad returned my hug, adding a kiss to the top of my head, but he directed his words to Frew. "What's up pal? You don't look too happy."

Frew shrugged. "To tell you the truth, it's pretty rotten to hear someone say those things about yourself. . . . But the other thing is that maybe I feel a bit guilty. You hardly know me, Mr. Vincent. I don't want you to go wrecking your business over me. It's not worth it."

Dad slung his arm over Frew's shoulder. "Son, I've had my priorities out of whack for too long. It's about time I got my life together. And besides, I've got a feeling I'd regret any business dealings I had with Frank Woods. Now let me change into some dry underwear"—he paused a moment to glare at Kate, who merely laughed—"and let's go eat!"

Going up the stairs, I asked Kate, "Is it me or is Dad really starting to relax? I've never seen him so loose! I sort of used to dream of messing around with him like today."

"Just be patient with him, Jo. He doesn't know how to let go and have fun. He's just learning."

"Is that why he and my mom didn't make a go of it?"

"I don't think it's my place to answer that."

"I'd like you to, Kate, please? Mom never says

anything bad about Dad, so I guess she'd never really tell me what happened."

I could see that this was a big decision for Kate. I guess she was weighing up my right to know and her right to tell me. I gave her my most pleading look. She sighed one of those I'm-going-to-regret-this sighs. "Well, according to your father, work became an obsession with him. It's taken him years to realize that he was the fault of the breakdown. He was angry, Jo, and he had to get over that anger before he could start to heal. That's why he had all those girlfriends. . . . Yes, don't look so surprised; he told me about them. In a way he was trying to hurt your mother. But he ended up hurting you and himself. Love him, Jo; he's got a long way to go."

"Jeez! You really are a saint!"

Kate laughed. "Oh, Jo! If only you knew! There's no way I'm anywhere near being a saint!"

I didn't care what she thought of herself; I still had my own ideas and I was sticking to them!

"Now, that's what I call a steak!" Dad leaned back and patted his stomach. He was thoughtful for a moment, just looking around the table at us all. "This is going to sound insensitive where you are concerned, Frewin, but I believe that this has been one of the best weeks of my life. I suppose it's been one of the worst in your life, huh?"

Frew reached under the table and squeezed my

hand. "Not entirely, Mr. V. It's had its high points."

I guess my dad isn't stupid; he caught on pretty quickly. He grinned at us both before declaring, "I think it might be time for a celebration! Have you ever had champagne, Jo? Frew? I don't think a little glass will hurt, do you, Kate?"

Kate seemed to look at Dad for a long time before answering. "Are you sure, Mal?" I had the distinct feeling that they weren't talking about underage drinking.

Dad nodded and ordered. While we were waiting, Dad surprised me by asking questions about the night the bracelet went missing. "And as far as any of you knew, no one came into the Chalet all night?" When we shook our heads he seemed really confused. "You know, something doesn't add up about this thing. If I could only put my finger on it. . . . everyone's room was searched. Seemingly no one but you and Frew were at the Chalet." He scratched his head. "Try to think, Kate! Was Cynthia wearing those diamond boulders when we were at dinner? Because if she was, then that puts a new light on the subject. Why didn't I ask that question before?"

I shouldn't have said it—it wasn't going to help now—but a part of me still burned that Frew was being treated so badly. "Maybe because you wanted to believe that you'd found the thief!" The guilty look that passed over Dad's face made me cringe. I hated myself at that moment; kicking Dad wasn't going to help anything. "I'm sorry, Dad; that was pretty low, but if what you·were saying is possible, then Frew couldn't possibly have done it. He was long gone by the time you all got home."

"Actually, they came home after us. We left a bit early."

"So you couldn't verify that Mrs. Woods had the bracelet on when she got home. She could have lost it when she was out!"

"She's right, Mal," Kate offered. "I wish I could actually remember if she had that darned thing on. I think she did, but I got so used to seeing it weighing down her wrist that I might just be imagining that I saw it."

"Mr. V, do you really think that there's a chance that we can prove that I didn't do it?"

"I don't know, Frewin, but I'm more hopeful now than I was an hour ago. Ah, the champagne. We have even more reason to celebrate now."

"More reason? What was the first reason?"

"Patience, Jo, patience," Dad warned as he poured the bubbly wine. "Now, everybody got a drink? Ahem, Jo . . ."

"Come on, Dad, cut the—"

"Jo! Just wait now; I'll get to it. It's not every day a man gets to make an announcement like this."

I felt all warm inside—I was ready. I'd guessed what was coming. Dad was obviously going to make some soppy speech about finding his daughter again. I had my smile in place; I guess I'd waited a long time for this moment.

"Ahem." Dad started again. "I hope you don't mind finding out this way, Jo, but we would like you two to be the first to know that I've asked Kate to marry me. And she has said yes."

My smile was frozen. All I could do was stare at the man. Marry? What ever happened to good old-fashioned de facto relationships? Where were his new-millennium values? The silence at the table was deafening.

"Jo?"

"Are you all right, sweetheart?"

I tried to get my brain to work; now if I could just coordinate my mouth. "S-sure. I . . . I hope you are hery vappy, I mean very happy."

Kate leaned over and pried my fingers from the stem of the champagne glass, which was obviously in danger of being crushed into a million pieces. "Jo, there is no easy way to say this. I love your father and I've come to love you. I want you to know that I will never try to be your mother, that I will always be your special friend, and that you will always come first with your dad. Whenever you need him he'll be there for you."

This afternoon I'd accepted that I was beginning to understand some of the problems between my parents. Now tonight I knew that there would never be a chance that they would get back together. There was a big difference from being told something and then being faced with absolute proof. Tonight was a special night for my father. For me it was a night to finally say good-bye to my childish dreams. A night to grow up. I leaned across and kissed Kate and then my dad. They were great about the fact that my tears were flowing all over them. My dad kept hold of my hand. He seemed to understand, and he hung on tight. Or was that me hanging tightly on to him? Whatever, my dad and I hung on to each other until I had it together again.

Back at the Chalet, Dad and Kate had gone to bed and it was just Frew and me. Franz had offered to be lookout in case any of the Woodses came prowling around. I was getting the feeling that no one liked the Woodses very much.

"It's been a pretty weird night, hasn't it?"

"What an understatement. It's going to take me a little while to get used to having a stepmother. It could have been heaps worse, though, I 'spose. Man! When I think of some of the bimbos that my father has taken out in the last few years . . ." I paused and shook my head, unable to imagine any of those being my stepmom. "At least Kate is really cool—I like her. I guess it's hard not to."

"I can't believe the way she and your old man

ran around the village after dinner asking every-body about Mrs. Woods's bracelet. What a crackup! They were like Sherlock Holmes and what's his name."

"Watson. Not that it did much good. No one seems to remember if she had it on. Actually," I went on, feeling lousier by the minute, "that prob-ably points to the fact that she probably *wasn't* wearing it."

The wind chose that moment to give a mournful howl, seeming to agree with our low moods. But it did give me a great excuse to cuddle in a little bit closer to Frew. The fire in the television room was starting to die down, and I knew that I'd have to go up to my room soon. Frew had wrapped both arms around me and was gently rubbing my back. This time there was nothing parental in the feelings he was giving me. I had to concentrate hard to keep my mind off those hands.

"I was really hoping we were going to find out something useful tonight. I feel so helpless, like here we are going home tomorrow afternoon and we're leaving you right in the middle of this mess!"

"We found out one thing, Jo." When I simply frowned he explained: "We found out that Justin has hang-ups about carrying his mother's purse!"

"Oh, yeah!" I gave a half laugh. "Not that it should have been a surprise; it goes with the ter-ritory when you're a chauvinist. What was it that the waitress said? That he got really ticked off when she remarked on the nice handbag he had under his coat? Something like that." My lousy mood returned. "Not that that fact is going to help us solve the mystery."

Frew's head was leaning against mine, his whispered words muffled by my hair. "Jo . . . let's forget about this rotten business for a while. You're going home tomorrow and I'm going to miss you like crazy."

By now the fire had completely gone out, and we both knew it was time for Frew to go home. Time for one last kiss good-bye. There was more than just sadness that we were going our separate ways; in a weird way I felt that I knew a little bit how people felt who were going off to war. Like how they didn't know what lay ahead of them. Poor old Frew must have felt like he was waiting for the jury to bring in a verdict, and me . . . well, maybe I just caught his feelings, but whatever, there was a funny, empty feeling to our last private good-bye.

"Meet me in the village straight after breakfast," I called as I pushed him through the door. "I want to make the most of tomorrow." His answer was another cute wink. Oh, I do looove being in looove . . . only this time it was hurting a lot too.

At the top of the stairs I bumped into Kate. "Where are you going?"

"To see if the kitchen is open; I can't sleep. Has Frew gone?"

"Yeah. How come you can't sleep?"

"This darned robbery! I think I've remembered something. All I'm worried about is that maybe my mind is playing tricks."

Excitement surging through me, I grabbed her by the hand. "Does it help Frew? Forget the kitchen! Quick, come into my room!" I was still firing questions at her as I dragged her to the beds and threw myself down onto one.

Kate sat down more slowly, obviously still trying to work things out. "Well, I only just remembered tonight that as I was coming out of my room on that night to go out to dinner, Cynthia was coming out of hers. She was just closing her handbag and was saying something about the clasp of something being stuck and that she'd put it on when she got out, after Frank had had a chance to look at it."

"Do you think she was talking about the bracelet? Because that would mean that she *did* have it with her and that she could have lost it anywhere! Especially if the clasp was dodgy!"

"Jo, don't get your hopes up. That woman wears so much jewelry that she could have been talking about anything."

"But Kate, let's pretend for argument's sake that she was talking about the bracelet. Okay, so her bracelet is razzed; she's going to get Frank-baby to fix it at the restaurant. So how does she take it there? Was she carrying anything in her hands? Did she have it in her pocket?"

"No, she wasn't carrying any jewelry, and Frank had that fur of hers over his arm. Bit risky if the bracelet was in the pocket. And the slinky outfit she wore didn't have anywhere for pockets."

"So," I interrupted, "the most obvious and only place left is that it was in her handbag! Kate, was every room in the Chalet searched?"

Kate's eyes were as bright as mine must have been. "I'm right with you, kiddo! No, not every room!"

I bounded off the bed and headed straight for the door.

"Where are you going?" she called.

"To search one of the rooms that wasn't searched!"

"Jo! You can't do that! It's called breaking and entering!"

"Kate, it's Frew's only chance! We *know* who stole that bracelet, but who'd believe us?"

Chapter Twelve

I didn't give my actions much thought; all I could see in my mind's eye was Kate and me barging into that room and finding the evidence. There was only one hitch: the door to Justin's room didn't budge. It was locked solid. And I didn't have time to take a course in picking locks.

Darn it! I slid down the wall, all the energy suddenly drained from me. Kate squatted beside me. "Jo, we're only surmising. . . . We don't know for sure, and we don't have any proof. Blaming Justin is as bad as everybody else blaming Frew without proof."

"But it all fits, Kate! He's a junkie. He'd need the money. When that waitress caught him with that bag, that wasn't embarrassment—it was guilt! He'd just stolen his mother's jewel!"

"Jo," Kate began patiently, "it sounds plausible,

but we still don't have any proof. Come on, let's go back to your room before someone catches us loitering and suspects *us!*"

Kate just about had to tie me down when we got to the room. I wanted to tear the place apart, I wanted to wake up Dad, I wanted to confront that slimy Justin, I wanted to do everything. I would have settled for anything! But Kate said that I would just make things worse, so I went to bed and did nothing.

Morning seemed to take forever coming. I guess I must have slept for some of the night, but most of it was spent trying to figure out a way to trap Justin. Unfortunately I couldn't think of one. Not one. Why isn't life like a television show? If it were then I would have thought of some brilliant plan by now.

I skipped breakfast, only shoving my head in through the dining room door to let Kate know that I hadn't run amok through the night, and took off to find Frew. I was a mass of mixed emotions; part of me wanted to go full steam ahead and get Justin busted, and yet another part of me wanted just to go slow, forget about everything except the fact that this was our last day together. Part of me was excited about being close to solving the mystery and part of me was sad that I was so far away from solving this darned mystery!

As soon as I saw Frew, I knew that I was just

going to relax and enjoy the next few hours, to try to stash away some great memories. That I was going to forget, at least for a while, about problems that I couldn't solve.

"Hi!" I mumbled after we'd shared a quick hug.

"Gidday! Aha! The trusty camera!"

"More than just the trusty camera, thank you. This piece of equipment is the beginning of my career in photojournalism, or if that fails then I might be forced to take my incredible talents and make a career on the stage."

Frew took the camera and started taking in the scenery through the viewfinder. "Isn't this where we came in? It was thanks to your absorption with this thing that we met."

I sighed dramatically. "Yes . . . I'll probably never flash again without thinking of you." I finished by fluttering my eyelashes like some lovesick heroine.

"Man, I hope you make it in the photo world. If that was a sample of your acting then I can see you starving!"

I snatched back the camera. "Hmph! Just for that I'll make you pose for two whole rolls—not just one!"

That mindless conversation set the tone for the rest of the morning. I snapped Frew in every bizarre position I could think of. We got other tourists to take a series of shots of us together, and Frew insisted on some of me alone, demanding a promise from me that I send the copies to him. Of course, I pretended to be really embarrassed while deep down I was cheering. I loved the idea of him showing all his mates back home photos of the real love of his life! Of course, once the *National Enquirer* got on the job, we'd have plenty of photos. . . .

If Frew could beat this trumped-up charge, that is . . . The thought was sobering. I think for a little while we also pretended that it all wasn't going to end in just a few hours.

"Just one more, Frew . . . there. If you move to the right just a bit then I can get those great chalets in the background. Hang on; you've gone too far. Now all I can see is that alleyway. Just . . ."

"Jo? Yoo-hoo . . . ? Earth calling Jo. Come on, am I in the right place or not?"

I could hear Frew's voice, but it seemed like it was coming from miles away. My attention was fixed on that alleyway. I could feel my heart start to beat faster. My fingers worked the telephoto lens as if on automatic pilot. I was grateful for their subconscious ability, because personally I was having trouble remembering how to breathe.

"Jo?" The voice was intruding again. In a distant part of my brain I registered that it was getting closer. I couldn't allow myself to concentrate on it; I wasn't game to blink. I prayed that Frew didn't walk across my sights. My position was perfect; the shot was clear and sharp . . . I waited, shaking and

breathless. The moment came, excitement over-
came nerves . . . I clicked again and again. I had it!

"Jo? What in the hell is the matter?"

I turned to Frew, the Frew whose innocence I had
just proved—not by any brilliant scheme, not by
any devious plan, but by sheer, old-fashioned good
luck. By some fluke we'd been in the right place at
the right time. I thought I was going to burst with
happiness! I grabbed him and threw my arms
around him in a hug that must have nearly suffo-
cated him. "We have to find Kate and Dad.
Quick!"

I couldn't blame the guy; I mean, he was looking
at me as if I'd gone off the deep end in a big way,
but I didn't have time to explain. I just dragged him
off toward the Chalet, hoping like hell that Dad
and Kate hadn't gone off on one of their mysterious trips.

Luck was still on our side, and I was thankful all
Dad and Kate were doing when we burst into their
room was packing!

"Oops! I know I should have knocked, Dad," I
apologized, rushing on before Dad could verbalize
the look of shock on his face. "But I have the proof!
I have the proof!"

"What in the devil are you talking about?" Dad
asked, still in shock.

"How did you get it?" That was Kate. "Are you
sure? You didn't break any laws, did you?"

"Break any laws? What in the heck is going on?"

"Cool down, Dad; it's okay. No, Kate." I turned to answer her section of the inquisition. "That's the most amazing part! I was just taking photos. It was a gift! I can't believe our luck."

"Jo, would you please just slow down and explain what is going on?"

I took a deep breath. "Okay, Dad, it's like this. Last night Kate and I worked out who we thought stole the bracelet, but we didn't have any proof. Just now, only a few minutes ago, I got that proof. I was taking photos of Frew when in the background I saw some action. I was curious, so I zoomed in on telephoto. Oh, man, this is so bizarre. . . ."

"Just tell us!" came a chorus from the other three, or something like that.

"Well, I saw this dodgy-looking guy in an alley, acting kind of suspicious, and then this other guy turned up from behind the Chalet. The first guy was obviously expecting the second guy and they started to argue. . . . Then the second guy pulled something out of his pocket and handed it to the first. He held it up to the light. Dad, Kate, Frew, I have photographs of Justin handing his mother's bracelet over to a guy I'd bet my life was a drug dealer! I have the proof!" I sat back, a smug smile on my face, and waited for it all to sink in. Was I brilliant or what!

The reactions were pretty predictable.

Dad: "Justin!"

Kate: "Are you sure?"

Frew: "Fair dinkum. Way to go! You little beauty!"

"Yes, Justin! Yes, I'm sure! And you are welcome!" I answered them all together. I'd had my fun; now it was down to the yucky bit. "Dad, we've only got a little while before we leave; you've got to get this mess cleared up for us. Do you, um . . . think you could go and break it to the Woods's?"

Dad looked like I'd just asked him to mud wrestle with a king cobra. "Are you absolutely sure about this, Jo? Kate?"

Kate answered. "There are other factors, Mal. I'd say that Justin is very much involved. And he does have a drug problem."

Dad sighed, dragging his hand through his hair. "A drug problem? Why didn't I see that?" He was still shaking his head. "Then I don't suppose I have a choice. All right, just wait here."

In the time that Dad was gone, none of us said very much. Our jubilation in proving that Frew was innocent wasn't as great as it seemed at first. We weren't really vindictive people—I guess rather than wanting to blame somebody else, we would have just preferred it hadn't happened at all.

The door opened, and Dad stood there just staring at us. None of us said anything at first, but then some things that had been nagging at the back of my brain suddenly clicked into gear. "They already knew, didn't they?" I whispered.

Dad stood there, tears shining in his eyes. He nodded. "Justin is in a lot of trouble. He's been expelled from college for academic misconduct. That means he was caught trying to pay someone to sit for some exams in his place. He's on a bond for drug use; that's why he's here with his folks instead of with his friends. They really wanted to believe that it wasn't him. They thought that if they could prove it was someone else then they wouldn't have to accept that the kid is in more trouble. I have just left two crushed parents. That has to rate as one of the hardest things I've ever done in my life. Frew, they send their apologies and they'll clear your name. I know it doesn't seem enough, but it's really all they can do. And I believe they will. If they don't we'll take care of it ourselves. But I don't think we have any concerns."

Kate turned to me, her face puzzled. "What made you think that they already knew, Jo?"

"I don't know, just little things. When Frew and I saw Mrs. Woods in the village, she said it didn't matter if she lost the bracelet because it was insured. And then they made this huge fuss. And then Frew said once that the Woodses were just looking for a 'fall guy.' At the time it rang a little bell, but it didn't make any sense till now. They were scared, weren't they? That's why they were so desperate to blame someone else. Thank heavens it's all over!"

Dad looked at his watch. "And just in time. Jo? We have to leave soon."

My face must have fallen, because good old Kate came to the rescue again. "If you like, Jo, I can pack for you. That'll give you a bit longer with Frew."

I didn't even answer; I just hugged her. "Come on, Frew. . . ."

We raced outside—back to the place it had all begun. Back to the very place where "Hans" had rescued me. Hans. What a hoot!

"I wish you didn't have to go, Jo."

"Me too. Maybe Dad will bring me back again sometime. Or you could come up to the West Coast. How about next summer? I could teach you to ride a surfboard."

He grinned. "That has a lot of possibilities. . . ."

I punched him in the arm, my face on fire. "I didn't mean *that*! You knew what I meant, you rat. You just like to see me suffer, don't you!"

Dad and Kate emerged from the Chalet with Franz and all our bags. "Come on, Jo, the airport coach is about to leave."

"Okay, Dad." I turned back to Frew. "Well, I guess this is it. . . ."

"I guess it is. Um, does this new relationship with

your dad stretch to having him cope with you being kissed in public? At least by me?"

"I don't know. Will we put him to the test?"

"Works for me . . ."

"Josephine!"

"Oops! Maybe he needs a bit more practice with the enlightened-dad bit. It's been a great week, Frew. Will you e-mail?"

"You bet. And Jo? I, um . . . really like you, if you know what I mean."

I knew what he meant.

"Me too."

It was sad—but suddenly I was feeling like myself again. I somehow knew it wasn't the end for us. Our friendship would last. Maybe even more . . . Besides, I hadn't starved myself for the last half of the week for the *National Enquirer* for nothing! On that thought I turned back to Frew. "Oh, and about the paparazzi? I think we should coordinate our 'good sides.' I'm not even sure which side *is* my good side yet—but I'll work on it. I just hope we're compatible—like at least facing each other! If we're always looking in opposite directions, people will talk!" I rolled my eyes at the horror. "Can you just see the headlines to accompany the photos?"

His face was a study in confusion. "What in the flamin' heck are you talking about?"

"Oh, der! The tabloids, of course! Keep up, Frew!"

"Jo, we have to leave!"

I started to blow Frew a kiss, but he turned to my dad in more confusion.

Dad just sighed. "Don't look at me, son. I've still got my learner's license where she's concerned."

I shook my head at all of them. Men! They'd work it out. Eventually.

Traveling on the coach I let my mind drift back over the week. And what a week it was. . . . Okay, I finally accepted I wasn't going to be called "Your Highness" and have someone to bring my low-fat crackers and diet Cokes on command. But I'd cope. And in truth, I wasn't sure that a royal wedding was really *me*. I wondered if they'd do the chicken dance. Probably not. And I bet the crown would be a loaner.

At the ladies' room at the airport I started practicing pouty, sexy, yet surprised facial expressions in the mirror. Okay, it might be a while, but I had to be ready for the cameras.

Trivialities aside, back in the lounge I admitted that it was really weird without Frew. Lonely. I missed him. Missed that grin. That accent. Those eyes that could be so understanding . . .

A thought suddenly hit me that Frew really might be the one big love of my life. That maybe that was it. And I'd had it. Passed it. Oh, no!

Didn't *YM* magazine do a survey that said love strikes only once and there's only one true person for everyone in the entire universe? Panic set in.

Even as our flight was called I was moving in a daze. That was it! *YM* mag was never wrong. There was no one else in the world for me. I'd never be in love again. I'd just left my one and only on the snow slopes, fighting back tears and waving a sad little wave. . . .

The flight attendant pointed out my seat and I robotically made my way to it. But as I sat down I knew I couldn't do it. I couldn't leave! I had to go back to Frew.

Blindly I tried to get back up, grasping at my hand luggage, not caring I was bashing other people in the head.

But I wasn't fast enough.

"*Scusi*—but is theeees seat fifty-nine B?" I looked up to the owner of the voice, my heart too heavy to answer—and then froze.

He was gorgeous. Absolutely heart-stoppingly gorgeous. *Be still, my beating heart.*

I nodded.

And then flopped back into my seat because my legs simply would not hold me up any longer.

Still smiling, he took my bag and shoved it up in the overhead compartment. Obviously I was staying. Then he settled and turned to me. "Please to meet you. I am Emilio."

"What a great accent!"

He smiled—and I figured it was at least five

hundred calories. Talk about sugar. And delicious!

"I'm Italian."

"You're Italian?"

"Sì!"

A goofy grin worked its way up and I could only stare. "How wonderful! I'm Jo, by the way." A little perplexed frown creased my forehead. "Um, do they have royalty in Italy?"

Suddenly the flight attendants checked our seat belts and it was time to take off. It was then I noticed a surfing logo on his jacket. I pointed to it. "You surf?"

He nodded again. *"Sì!"*

It was a sign. . . .

I smothered a grin by turning to the window. It was snowing lightly. Wonderful. Idly, I turned back to Emilio's hot-chocolate eyes. Perhaps the flight would be delayed or diverted for a few hours. I for one would be the perfect passenger and not utter one word of complaint.

My cell phone burned in my pocket. Would I be able to use it in flight? Wishing I could get a shot of this hunk, I suddenly knew just what I wanted for my birthday: a cell phone with photo transmission. A girl just never knew when an opportunity was going to sit right down beside her. . . .

My sigh came from the deepest part of my soul.

Every girl should have at least one Frew in her life. But then again, if her heart is breaking then there's nothing like an Emilio to make her feel better.

He smiled again.

Maybe I'd be better at Italian than I'd been at German and French.

"Emilio? What's the Italian word for 'princess'?"

Epilogue

To: Jo Vincent <surferjo@freemail.com>
From: Frewin Philpott <wingold@olympicsRus.com>
Subject: Italian woman stealers

Gidday, Jo! Your last mail was really great! Maybe you should become a writer instead of a photographer. Bit worried about this Emilio bloke, tho. Should I be jealous?

Frew.

To: Frewin Philpott <wingold@olympicsRus.com>
From: Jo Vincent <surferjo@freemail.com>
Subject: Royal wanna-bes

Emilio? Boooring. Jeez, Frew! How could you even think I'd look at another guy? He was just someone to yap to on the flight. All he wanted to do was talk about himself. And he knows absolutely zilch about surfing! He was a real poser! BTW, did you know there's no real royal family in Italy? They were deposed or something. Sounds painful, whatever it is. Anyway, I could tell a mile off that he didn't have any royal blood. It's a gift I have. Gotta go. Dad's got me a German tutor. I think he has plans to do biz with the Germans and he's worried I'll blow it for him.

P.S. Don't worry—*her* name is Gerda! LOL!

P.P.S. Help! I can't believe I forgot to ask about your trip back home! Oh, der!!!

Really miss you,

Jo xxxxxxxx

To: Jo Vincent <surferjo@freemail.com>
From: Frewin Philpott <wingold@olympicsRus.com>
Subject: Home visit

Gidday! Home was great. Made me realize how much I miss them all. Dad and the bros were giving me a hard time about my American sheila. Tried to tell 'em we're just mates—but they're not really listening. I think they're having too much fun to listen. I'm a prime target.

The old man was waiting for me. In five days he made me help him fix two motors and three gearboxes! The bros reckon he's wrecking them just so he's got the chance to lecture me.

At least he's given up on the sex-education basics. Now it's worse—now he's on about marriage and families and responsibilities! Man, I think he's trying to scare the hell out of me. If that's his plan, it's working! I keep telling him that I'm only seventeen, but he keeps telling me that you're never too young to learn.

I haven't got any idea where this is all coming from. You haven't been talking to him, have you? LOL!

Miss you back,
Frew

To: Frewin Philpott <wingold@olympicsRus.com>
From: Jo Vincent <surferjo@freemail.com>
Subject: Kisses

Hi—why don't you ever send me any kisses? I always send you kisses!

Miss you more,
Jo xxxxxxxxxxx

To: Jo Vincent <surferjo@freemail.com>
From: Frewin Philpott <wingold@olympicsRus.com>
Subject: California, here I come!

It was a real buzz to get that invitation and air ticket to your dad and Kate's wedding. It looks like I'll be able to make it, but I'll only be able to stay for the weekend. I'm pretty freaked out about meeting your mum, though—put in a few good words for me, huh?

Miss you most,

Frew

To: Jo Vincent <surferjo@freemail.com>
From: Frewin Philpott <wingold@olympicsRus.com>
Subject: Your dad is the greatest!

Wow!!!! I just got a call from your dad! He's organizing some sponsorship for me! Says he's been planning some deal with this big company and they're ready to interview me. Can you believe that? Says he'll talk to me at the wedding and can I swing an extra few days to fit in the interview. Can I?!

Can you believe that? He is one really cool dude!

And kisses? Work it out.

Still miss you,

Frew!

To: Frewin Philpott <wingold@olympicsRus.com>
From: Jo Vincent <surferjo@freemail.com>
Subject: Kisses—last time

Great! But what about the kisses! Work out what?

Jo (Missing you but not sure she wants to send you any more . . . kisses, that is.)

To: Jo Vincent <surferjo@freemail.com>
From: Frewin Philpott <wingold@olympicsRus.com>
Subject: Kisses

Okay, Nerf brain! Haven't you worked it out yet? I'm saving them for the real thing. . . .
Frew—counting the days.

To: Frewin Philpott <wingold@olympicsRus.com>
From: Jo Vincent <surferjo@freemail.com>
Subject: Lethal kisses

Hi, Frew. This is Cassie—Jo's friend. I'm sending this reply 'cause when Jo read your reply about the "real thing" she did this really stoopid swoon thing and banged her head against the open closet door and she had to get a couple of teeny stitches. She says to tell you not to worry—that she's fine. Just got a headache.

And that she's gonna have a teeny, tiny scar. So she really needed you to know urgently that she now has a bad side. It's her left—so you'll always have to remember to walk on her right. Okay? It's about the paparazzi. She said you'd understand.
Cassie

P.S. How old are your brothers?
P.P.S. Do they ever come for a visit?
P.P.P.S. Jo says she misses you.

To: Jo Vincent <surferjo@freemail.com>
From: Frewin Philpott <wingold@olympicsRus.com>
Subject: Lethal kisses

Jo! Are you okay? Cassie's e-mail really sent me for a spin!

And man—what *is* it with this paparazzi thing? Help me! I'm clueless here!

Wait a minute . . . I'm just sitting here thinking. All that royal stuff. They were clues, right? Oh, jeez, Jo . . . are you, like, royal or something? Are you trying to prepare me? I gotta tell you it's freaked me right out. I dunno how to tell you this, but, like, I think that stuff is a giant turnoff.

I really can't see me sitting around drinking tea and eating oatmeal cookies with the queen or anything. Besides, I'm allergic to Corgis. . . .

Not long till I see you,
Frew

To: Frewin Philpott <wingold@olympicsRus.com>
From: Jo Vincent <surferjo@freemail.com>
Subject: Lethal kisses

Hi, Frew . . . I'm okay—and I gotta admit that maybe that knock to the head has finally kicked some sense in. No, I'm not royal, so you can relax. And you know what? I've finally realized all that stuff is a turnoff, too. So false. So public! So tacky.

From now on it's just gonna be ordinary Frew and ordinary Jo. Okay? I'm feeling much better about it already. I'd better go; I still have to rest a bit. Hang on—just noticed some new people moving in next door. See? I'm ordinary. Suburban. Just an ordinary neighbor being curious . . . How ordinary can I get!

I can see this woman. Nice 'do! Kinda Meg Ryan style. And a kid. Little kid. And this guy. He's turning toward the window. . . . Oh, my God! Can you believe who has just moved in next door!!! Oh, my God! It's that . . . that movie director! What's his name? You know the one! It's a sign, Frew! I tell you, it's a sign!

Gotta go! Gotta beat Cassie to meet him! Gotta hide my scar!!!

See ya next weekend!

Jo (Watch for that name in the movies!!!! Oooohhhhhh!)

The Year My Life Went Down the Loo
by Katie Maxwell

Subject: The Grotty and the Fabu (No, it's not a song.)
From: Mrs.Oded@btelecom.co.uk
To: Dru@seattlegrrl.com

Things That Really Irk My Pickle About Living in England

- The school uniform
- Piddlington-on-the-weld (I will forever be known as Emily from *Piddlesville*)
- Marmite (It's yeast sludge! GACK!)
- The ghost in my underwear drawer (Spectral hands fondling my bras—enough said!)
- No malls! What are these people *thinking???*

Things That Keep Me From Flying Home to Seattle for Good Coffee

- Aidan (*Hunkalicious!*)
- Devon (*Droolworthy?* Understatement of the year!)
- Fang (He puts the *num* in *nummy!*)
- Holly (Any girl who hunts movie stars with me—and Oded Fehr *will be mine*—is a friend for life.)
- Über-coolio Polo Club (Where the snogging is FINE!)

They Wear WHAT Under Their Kilts?

by Katie Maxwell

Subject: Emily's Glossary for People Who Haven't Been to Scotland
From: Mrs.Legolas@kiltnet.com
To: Dru@seattlegrrl.com

Faffing about: running around doing nothing. In other words, spending a month supposedly doing work experience on a Scottish sheep farm, but really spending days on Kilt Watch at the nearest castle.

Schottie: Scottish Hottie, also known as Ruaraidh.

Mad schnoogles: the British way of saying big smoochy kisses. Will admit it sounds v. smart to say it that way.

Bunch of yobbos: a group of mindless idiots. In Scotland, can also mean sheep.

Stooshie: uproar, as in, "If Holly thinks she can take Ruaraidh from me without causing a stooshie, she's out of her mind!"

Sheep dip: not an appetizer.

Available in January 2004.

Amy Kaye

THE REAL DEAL

Focus on *THIS!*

Caught on tape: The newest reality television series goes on location somewhere truly dangerous—high school. Outrageous and unscripted, each episode exposes the sickest gossip, finds the facts behind the rumors, and bares the raw truth. Tune in and take it all in, because no subject is too taboo, no secret too private, and no behavior off limits!

Meet Fiona O'Hara—stuck in a suburban sitcom a million light-years away from her native New York City, a.k.a. civilization. Her mom is a basket case since the divorce. Her dad is Mr. Disappearo. And the one guy who seems like a decent love-interest has a psycho wannabe girlfriend who's ready to put a hit out on her.

Didn't want this book to end?

There's more waiting at **www.smoochya.com**:

Win FREE books and makeup!
Read excerpts from other books!
Chat with the authors!
Horoscopes!
Quizzes!